I Married a Billionaire

Melanie Marchande

DEDICATION

For my husband.

CONTENTS

ACKNOWLEDGMENTS

This book would certainly not exist in its current form without the tireless help and advice of everyone involved in the Insatiable Reads Book Tour. Special thanks are due to Jordan, Erika, Tanya, Carré, and Anya.

I also owe an incredible debt of gratitude to all those who helped put me on this path to my dream job of writing for a living. Much love to Delilah and everyone at BFC and EWS. I wouldn't be here without you.

Chapter One

When your billionaire boss's attorney contacts you out of the blue, your first instinct is to assume something is horribly wrong and that you're about to pay the price. I still remember the way my throat tightened, the sweat on my palms - what was it about? I was sure I'd done nothing wrong, but if Mr. Thorne decided I had, there wasn't much recourse.

My boss was notoriously difficult to work for. Thankfully, I rarely saw him. At most he was a vaguely menacing presence in the corner of my eye; a whiff of expensive cologne as he passed by my desk. To him I was surely no more than a line on the payroll sheets that he blindly signed every quarter; I wasn't even confident that he knew my name.

And I liked it that way. I'd had overinvolved, micromanaging bosses before, and I much preferred a cold distant figure that I didn't even have to speak to. I worked hard - I didn't need someone hanging over my shoulder to make sure I was doing everything right.

As one of the graphic designers, I reported directly to Lisa, the head of Creative. She was pleasant enough, but I'd never gotten any feedback from her other than a nod of acknowledgement when I showed her my mockups and designs. Quite a few of them made it onto marketing and training materials, so I assumed Mr. Thorne liked my work.

So when a man approached me in the hallway and introduced himself as Mr. Thorne's attorney, the only thought that popped into my head was that I had somehow unwittingly committed copyright or trademark infringement, costing the company millions of dollars, and I would be fired on the spot. Or perhaps I'd accidentally incorporated something obscene into one of my designs...

"Mr. Thorne would like to see you about a special project."

I snapped out of my panic mode.

"A...project?"

I must have sounded skeptical, because he went on: "It's very important. A logo redesign for the company. He wants to keep it quiet for the meantime, but he asked to speak to you specifically."

I was torn between flattery, and a curious sense of foreboding. I was proud of myself, of course, for attracting his attention. Then again, the attention of a man like that might be something I'd regret having in the very near future.

"Right now?" was all I could muster, for all the thoughts swirling in my brain.

"Yes," said the attorney. "Right now."

I followed him down the long hallway that led to Mr. Thorne's office. It was separated from the rest of us by enough distance to make him seem untouchable. I wondered if he'd learned about that in one of his many management conferences.

I hesitated at the door. I'd never been inside his office before. Aside from Lisa, I didn't know anyone here who had. I felt like the attorney would soon ask me to take off my shoes, or perform some act of contrition.

Instead, he simply pushed the door open and walked in, gesturing for me to follow.

The office was not at all what I expected. I would have imagined it as something Spartan and cold, with a lot of empty space, no human touch whatsoever. Instead, the first thing that caught my eye when I walked in was the variety of tropical plants thriving around Mr. Thorne.

Some were clustered by the window, some featured in a small alcove against the back wall, and a few small ones even lived on his massive mahogany desk. The multitude of grow lights gave the office a soft, welcoming glow. The ceiling, too, was just the right height - not so tall that the space was forbidding, but not so low that it felt stuffy and cramped.

Mr. Thorne himself stood in the center of the room, by a grouping of lounge chairs and a small coffee table. He was smiling guardedly. Or maybe that was just his normal smile. I didn't think I'd ever looked at him fully in the face before, and I'd certainly never seen him smile. It made him look younger. Not that he'd looked *old* before, but the difference was marked. I actually had no idea about his age, but I'd always guessed him to be in his early thirties.

"Please, Ms. Wainwright," he said, gesturing towards one of the chairs. "Take a seat. Can I offer you something to drink? Coffee? Water? Juice?"

I shook my head.

"Before we begin, I want to assure you that this meeting is absolutely nothing to be concerned about. I have no issues with your job performance here. I have a business proposal for you, which I believe to be mutually beneficial. My attorney is here to oversee our negotiations and ensure that each of us is getting a fair deal. Do you follow so far?"

I nodded, swallowing hard. I suspected he was about to ask me to do something that was against every business ethics seminar I'd ever been forced to sit through.

He took a seat in one of the chairs opposite me, unbuttoning his suit jacket. "I want you to understand that if you refuse, your employment here would not be jeopardized in any way."

The attorney was twirling his pen between two fingers, staring at the floor. I got the feeling he wasn't very happy with what was going on, but he wasn't about to say anything as long as he was getting his paycheck.

"Ms. Wainright, as I'm sure you know, I've been living and working in this country for a long time. This place is my home. This is where I have built everything that's important to me. But, as it happens, I was born just across the border, in Toronto. Unfortunately, I put my trust in the wrong person to handle the paperwork that should have allowed me to legally live and work here. He stole a lot of money from me, but worse than that, he failed to properly file my papers. I was not aware of this until I received notice from the INS that I was no longer welcome here." He paused, fiddling with his cufflinks. "You're an intelligent woman, I'm sure you can see where this is going."

Well. This certainly had taken an interesting turn.

I forced myself to think about this logically, if such a thing were possible. He was a good-looking guy, of course - no question about that - in fact, I couldn't help but think I'd look slightly dingy by comparison, on his arm. But obviously he didn't think so. Or he didn't care.

I cleared my throat. "Mr. Thorne...sir...can I ask why you picked me?"

He looked at me for a moment. "Your supervisor," he said, finally. "Mrs. Anderson. Lisa. She's one of the few people who know about my...problem. When she came to me and told me that you and she had several conversations where you expressed distaste for the institution of marriage, I thought you might be interested."

"That's - quite a leap of logic," I said, frowning at him. If I'd known Lisa was practically in Mr. Thorne's pocket, I never would have had so many deeply personal conversations with her. She'd just gone on maternity leave, so I wouldn't even have an opportunity to corner her and ask her what the hell she was thinking. Not that I'd dare. I tried to think of other things I'd said to her, my ears starting to burn as I searched my mind.

Mr. Thorne bit his lip. "I've offended you,"

he said, standing up. "I apologize."

"Wait," I said. "Are you serious about this?"

"Yes," he said. "Of course."

"You're not playing some kind of elaborate prank on me?"

His smile returned. "What sort of person do you think I am?"

The attorney made a small noise, shifting in his chair.

"I assume I'll be compensated in some way?" I said, trying to sound cool and composed. I didn't know the proper way to react in this situation - hell, I didn't know if there *was* a proper way - but I was trying to pretend like he hadn't completely floored me with this offer. A marriage of convenience? Who even did that in real life?

"Of course," said Mr. Thorne, sitting back down and reaching for the sheaf of papers sitting on the table. "It's quite simple, when you cut through all the legalese. You will need to live with me for the next year, at least, for appearance's sake. During that time, I will support you and provide for all of your needs and wants. After that time passes, you will be compensated with two million dollars U.S., payable in cash or bearer bonds."

My heart stopped for a moment.

Mr. Thorne didn't skip a beat. "You will need to end your employment here, obviously -

again, for appearance's sake. But I will ensure that you receive an even better job placement at another firm, after the terms of the agreement are fulfilled. In the event of any legal trouble, you will still be compensated, so long as you make a reasonable effort to keep the façade intact."

"What constitutes a reasonable effort?" I wanted to know.

He rustled some pages. "That's spelled out here, as well. You're agreeing to spend a minimum of ten hours going over the details of our fictional relationship in preparation for the INS interview. When in public, you will behave at all times as if we are a couple. This may include some physical interaction, which..." he drifted off, staring at the carpet. Was he embarrassed? Surely not. "...I hope you will find...agreeable..."

The attorney sighed loudly. "I feel compelled to point out that a contract for an illegal agreement will not hold up in court."

I hadn't even considered that, but of course he was right.

Mr. Thorne nodded. "The contract is a formality. Just to clarify the obligations we'd both have."

"It sounds...." I wasn't sure how it sounded. "Can I have some time to think about it?"

"Excellent," said Mr. Thorne, briskly, his

professional demeanor returning in a moment's time. I noticed there was still some extra color in his face, though. "You can peruse the contract as thoroughly as you'd like, but I'm afraid I can't allow it to leave this room. For obvious reasons."

"Of course," I said. I flipped through the pages, my eyes scanning the words as if I could possibly make sense of them. My head was swimming, and I felt like I was in some kind of dream. Some part of me was convinced that I would wake up at any moment.

"You can take a few days, if you like." said Mr. Thorne. " Come to my office anytime if you want to look over it. I'll keep it in my desk."

"Thank you," I said. "I think I'll come back tomorrow."

He nodded, taking the papers from me and straightening them. "I'll see you then."

I spent the rest of my work day in a haze. Two million dollars? If I played my cards right, with the lifestyle I was accustomed to, I could live off of that money forever. Probably. Couldn't I? I actually had no idea; I'd never considered the possibility of having a few million dollars dropped in my lap. I had fantasies, of course. Didn't everyone? But I had never given them any serious thought.

I supposed I could hire someone to manage the money. Mr. Thorne probably knew some reputable financial planners - people who would make sure that I never had to work another day in my life. I could pursue my art on my own terms, instead of toiling away as a corporate drone for the rest of my working years.

Whoa, Maddy. Step back a minute.

My brain was already churning as if I had the money in my bank account. But if I decided to do this - and that was a huge *if* - it would still be a long time before I saw a dime. And in the meantime, living with Mr. Thorne, I'd probably get used to a higher standard of living. Even for someone like me, who'd never been pampered in my life, it would be difficult to go back to normal. I would be best if I could consult with some neutral third party about all of this - a professional. Someone who could give me some really solid advice. But I was pretty sure I'd have to pay handsomely for that, and I didn't exactly have Daniel Thorne money.

Yet.

-

Sitting up in bed that night, with no hope of sleeping, I finally got a pen and paper and began to write down a list of questions and concerns. Part of me couldn't believe that I was taking his offer seriously, but how could I not?

I dragged myself out of bed the next

morning after a few hours of fitful sleep. When I got to work, I made a beeline for Mr. Thorne's office.

I stopped at his assistant's desk. She looked at me with barely restrained contempt.

"I need to see Mr. Thorne," I said. "About the special project. He told me to stop by anytime."

Her lips thinned as she pressed the button on the intercom.

"Mr. Thorne. Ms. Wainright is here to see you."

"Thank you, please send her in."

I walked in slowly, shutting the padded door behind me. I was sure he'd look up when I came to a stop in front of his desk, but his head stayed down as she shuffled through a pile of paperwork.

I cleared my throat.

"Ms. Wainright," he said, blinking. "Good morning. You're very...early."

I frowned a little. "I get here at this time every day."

"Of course," he said, beginning to collect himself into the smooth professional that I somewhat recognized. "Please. Take a seat."

I sat down in the chair across from his desk, clutching my notepad to my chest. "I just have a few questions about the proposed arrangement," I said. "I can come back later if this is a bad time."

"No, no, not at all," he said. "Please. Go on."

I stared at my paper. The questions all sounded stupid now that I was in front of him, under his piercing green stare. But somewhere in the rational portion of my mind, I knew that they were still important. I swallowed hard and then began to speak.

"There's only one copy of the contract, right? Who will keep it?"

Mr. Thorne answered quickly. "Excellent question. My attorney, Mr. Wegman, is responsible for keeping the document private and secure. I realize this may sound like a conflict of interest, since I'm paying him, but I assure you that he will be representing us both equally in this arrangement. I made certain to add the terms of his payment into the contract as well, so he is highly motivated to keep it safe."

"During the term of our marriage, while I'm...living with you." I hesitated. "I understand that I'm supposed to act like your wife. Will there be any other restrictions or expectations on my behavior that I should be aware of?"

"None whatsoever," said Mr. Thorne. "So long as you appear to be in love with me, and faithful, I see no reason why you shouldn't be able to live the rest of your life as you choose." He hesitated.

God, this was so weird. My mouth was incredibly dry. "You said you'll be supporting me. Will I have a daily allowance, or...?"

"My credit card," he said, easily. "There is no limit. You'll be added as a joint member on the account and have your own card. You may use it to pay for anything you like. You see, Ms. Wainright, this whole arrangement requires a mutual trust. But in the time you've been employed here, I've seen no reason to believe that you are dishonest or that you take undue advantage of situations. That's one of the other reasons I chose you."

I looked up from my paper. "I thought you chose me because I don't believe in marriage."

He laced his fingers together thoughtfully. "That was the deciding factor," he said. "But I had already evaluated your character."

He was talking about me like I was a set of characteristics rather than a person. Then again, I supposed that came with the territory. Being a successful businessman meant coldly evaluating situations, completely devoid of any emotional impulses. It meant reading people like they were a string of zeroes and ones who happened to have an organic brain rather than one made of chips and diodes.

It must be liberating, to not have to worry about other people's feelings.

But perhaps that was best. If I was going to

enter into a marriage of convenience, it really ought to be with someone who was going to keep things professional and break it off at the end without any messiness.

And pay me a whole truckload of money, of course. That was a nice bonus.

"There was something else I wanted to address with you," he said, looking down at the desk. "I meant to bring it up yesterday. If, during the term of our marriage, you were to meet someone..."

"I'm not worried about that," I interrupted, quickly.

He looked up at me, his eyes searching my face. It seemed like I'd succeeded in reminding him that I was, in fact, a human being. "Are you certain about that?"

"Yes," I said. "Can we move on?"

"Of course," he said. "That brings me to my next point. It's important that we keep things professional. With an arrangement like this, sometimes the lines can become blurred. But I hope we can both act as checks and balances against each other to ensure that things stay appropriate. You're clearly a sensible person, so I don't anticipate this being too much of a problem. But it would be foolish to pretend we're not human beings." He gave me a sharp look, like he'd been reading my mind. I fidgeted. "If you feel things are becoming too personal, please don't hesitate to let me know. And I will do the same for you."

I nodded, trying to ignore the uncomfortable prickling at the base of my neck. It almost felt like he was looking through me.

He was silent for a while, and I realized he was waiting for some sort of verbal acknowledgement.

"Yeah," I said. "Of course, that...that sounds good," I said, my voice cracking a little. I realized belatedly that I was making it sound like I'd already consented to the arrangement, and briefly panicked. "I mean - if I decide to go through with this."

"Of course," he said, raising both hands in a supplicating gesture. "Nothing is official until we both sign the contract in the presence of my attorney."

"Sorry," I said. "I just wanted to make sure you weren't misunderstanding me."

He smiled. "I'm a very cautious man, Ms. Wainright. I'm not in the habit of making assumptions until I have signatures in triplicate."

"Well, that's good to know." I stood up. "Thank you, Mr. Thorne. I appreciate your time."

"I ought to be thanking you," he said, rising as well and extending his hand for me to shake. "Take as much time as you need. I have a few months before they'll loose the hounds, so it's not terribly urgent."

I had to laugh. "I appreciate that, but I don't think I'll be able to sleep properly until I make a decision." *And maybe not even then.*

He looked a little bothered. "I never meant to cause you any distress," he said. "I meant it when I said that refusing wouldn't impact your career. You can continue to work here as long as you like. You'll be treated like any other employee. And if you choose to leave I will always give you a positive reference. You have my word."

"I know," I said. "It's not that. I just...I guess I can't decide if the risk is worth the reward."

He considered this for a moment. "I won't pretend there isn't a risk," he admitted, finally. "But...it is not as great of a risk as you might think. I am in...an advantageous position."

My eyes narrowed. "What does that mean, exactly?"

Mr. Thorne shrugged a little. "Money opens many doors, Ms. Wainwright. As I'm sure you know."

"If it's a question of money, why do you need me at all?"

"I said 'many' doors. Not every door."

"Fair enough," I said. "I'll get back to you when I'm made my decision."

"Thank you," he said. "Again. For

everything."

Chapter Two

By the end of the week, I'd chewed every single fingernail down to the nubbins.

Every time I considered asking someone for advice - even anonymously on the Internet - a wave of paranoia would overtake me, and I'd bite my tongue. I couldn't risk doing anything that would violate Mr. Thorne's trust in me. Even if I hadn't signed the contract yet, if I did, I was pretty sure the silence clause would apply retroactively. Or would it?

I found myself wishing that I could afford my own lawyer. It would be helpful to go over this whole thing with someone who was level-headed and experienced, and who could be trusted to keep things quiet. But that simply wasn't possible.

Driving home on Friday, I was completely drained. And for the first time in a while, a weekend of quiet relaxation simply wasn't in the cards - I was going to spend the whole break mulling this situation over in my head, trying to figure out my next move. Whatever decision I made was certainly one I'd have to live with, well, for the rest of my life.

I became dimly aware of a rattling noise

coming from somewhere, but I tried to ignore it as I approached the world's longest traffic light. I wasn't sure if it was really longer than others or if it just seemed like it was, because it was only a few blocks from my apartment. But either way, I gritted my teeth when I saw it turn red as I approached.

The rattling noise grew louder as I idled. I tapped my knuckles against the dashboard, hoping it was some loose piece of something that didn't matter. The car was getting old, after all.

The rattling turned into a grinding noise, and as I let off the brake and pushed down on the accelerator, I felt the car lurch to a start, right before it ground to a sickening halt in the middle of the intersection.

Yes.

Perfect.

-

I could feel my back begin to ache as I sat at the mechanic's, in a tiled room that stank of oil and rubber. Beside me, on the table, there was a stack of four-year-old magazines that were badly wrinkled and smeared with grease. I couldn't shake the feeling of dread. I just knew the news wasn't going to be good, and there was no way I could afford a major repair right now.

When they finally called me up to the counter, I could barely focus on what they were saying to me. The few words that penetrated the haze in my brain didn't sound good. "Badly degraded." "Major repairs." "Payment plan."

Numbly, I pulled out the only credit card I had that wasn't already maxed out and handed it over to make my first deposit. If I lived off of cup noodles for a while, I could manage to make the minimum payments. Hell, if I was lucky, I 'd only be paying this off until I retired.

Of course, there was another option.

As I rode the courtesy shuttle home, I lost myself in a fantasy of being a billionaire's bride. Even if it was just for a year...of course I'd have my payment after that, which would be a dream come true in and of itself. But to live for an entire year, without having to think or worry about money once? That was beyond anything I could even imagine. Once I was managing my own small fortune, it would be different. I'd be worried about where to invest it, how to save it - I'd spend all of my free time concerned with making it last. But while I was playing the role of Mr. Thorne's wife, I'd be completely worry-free. If I needed anything - anything at all - I could have it.

I was tired of this life. I was exhausted from living paycheck to paycheck, trying to scrape enough money together to float my credit card bills for another month. Between my student loan payments and some old medical bills, most of my paychecks left my hands before I even had a chance to think about where to spend them.

But it didn't have to be that way anymore.

Mr. Thorne had given me his personal cell phone number - something that I suspected he rarely gave to anyone. He was anxious to know my decision. Of course he was. He tried to hide it as best he could, but I knew how badly he needed me to say yes.

When I got home, I pulled the wrinkled sticky note out of my pocket and dialed the number.

He answered on the first ring.

"Hello?" His voice was dark and smooth, like...no, I couldn't let myself think that way. *Come on, Maddy. Get it together.*

"Hello, Mr. Thorne? It's uh...it's Madeline Wainright."

There was just a moment's hesitation. "I think maybe...you ought to get used to calling me Daniel." I could hear him smiling down the phone. The fact that I was calling him out of the blue gave away my hand.

"Okay, Daniel," I said. "Have the contract ready for me on Monday."

"Of course," he said.

"I know it's a purely verbal agreement at this point, but can you do something for me?"

"Anything."

I felt goose bumps rising on my arms, for some incomprehensible reason.

"I'll need a ride to work," I said. "My car broke down, and it's going to be in the shop for at least a week..."

"Of course, Madeline. I'll send a town car to pick you up Monday morning. And don't worry about paying for the repairs, I'll see that it's done. Did you take it to Fellman's?"

"How did you know?"

"Lucky guess." I could hear him shuffling some papers. "I'll see you on Monday, Madeline."

"Yeah, see you later." Why were my ears burning? I dropped the phone on the sofa and went to run myself a hot bath. I needed to sink into oblivion for a moment; the decision I'd just made was too big to even think about rationally until I'd had some rest.

As I dropped my clothes into the hamper in the hallway and walked naked to the bathroom, I started to think about how awkward it would be to live with Mr. Thorne. With Daniel. We were basically strangers. Despite our charade, it wasn't like I was about to walk around naked in front of him. I'd been living by myself for so long that I was used to being in a certain amount of privacy when I was home. Being around someone all the time would definitely take some adjusting-to.

Of course, I'd still be alone during the day, when he was at work. That was another thing I hadn't really considered. What would it be like, living a life where I wasn't obligated to go anywhere or do anything? Aside from the fancy dinners and restaurants I assumed I'd be expected to attend on Daniel's arm, I'd have all the free time in the world. What on earth was I going to do?

I kept forgetting that money was no object. As I sank into the steaming water, I remembered that I could go back and take those figure drawing classes I'd always wanted to do, but never found the time for. Hell, I could take private lessons. I could drop all this commercial crap and only create the kind of art that would make somebody's soul sing...

I had to stop and laugh at myself. I was getting way, way ahead of things. I still had to adjust to the idea of being someone's wife, even if it was only temporary.

From what little I knew of Daniel, I was sure he had the whole thing planned out. He knew already what our first kiss would be like, where he'd spontaneously propose, and when we'd impulsively run over to Vegas or the judge's offices to get married, or whatever. He was already planning the first time he'd put his hand on my lower back, signaling to the whole world that I belonged to him. And I couldn't quite decide if I hated that idea, or loved it - maybe a little more than I should.

Even in the hot water, I shivered.

I wasn't about to question the business plans of such a successful man, but I had to wonder how believable our relationship would appear to be. I wasn't exactly the sort of glamorous supermodel type that the richest of the rich tended to marry. He'd made it pretty clear that he wasn't expecting me to act a certain way, but how would I be expected to dress? I'd never seen Daniel in anything but a suit; then again, I'd never seen him outside of work.

The full absurdity of my situation hit me then, and for a moment I felt lightheaded with panic. Then I remembered that I hadn't actually signed anything yet, and I calmed down slightly. Just slightly. There still a part of my brain that knew I wasn't going to go back on my word. I wouldn't be able to handle the disappointment on his face.

-

Sure enough, the town car was there at seven a.m. sharp. I'd been waiting out on the curb, not wanting to be rude and make the driver wait. He seemed surprised when he saw me.

"Good morning," he said. "I would have called up for you, there's no need to wait."

"Oh, sorry." Of course. A couple days into this fake relationship, and I was already bungling things. "I'm not really familiar with...this whole thing."

"No, no, it's all right," he insisted. "I just thought you should know, for tomorrow."

"Tomorrow?" I looked up at his face reflected in the rearview. "I only asked for a ride today." But come to think of it, I hadn't considered how I'd get to work for the rest of the week.

"Mr. Thorne said you would require my services at least until Friday," he replied. "Is that not right?"

"Oh, no, that's...that's fine."

I stared out the window as he pulled away. Daniel was already making an effort to anticipate my needs. It was rather sweet of him, although I could see the potential for it to get pretty creepy and controlling. Then again, the contract pretty much spelled out that he wasn't allowed to dictate most parts of my life...I chuckled a little, wishing I'd signed a contract at the beginning of my relationship with all my boyfriends. Probably would have eliminated the worst ones right off the bat.

I stopped by my desk briefly when I got into

work, to drop off my coat and purse before I headed to Daniel's office. Florence, my cubicle mate, was already there.

"Where are you off to so early?" she asked, seeing me puttering around with no obvious intention of settling in.

"Oh, I have to see Mr. Thorne," I replied, trying to keep my face neutral. I'd probably look like I was hiding something, but that would fit in nicely with the fictional progression of our relationship.

"You've been spending a lot of time in his office lately," Florence observed, her eyes glued on her computer screen. "I swear to God, if GreatReads doesn't stop sending me these notification emails...how many times do I have to turn them off?"

"See you," I called over my shoulder as I hurried off, convincingly playing the part of a woman who's embarrassed to be carrying on with her boss. It wasn't too much of a stretch.

Daniel was smiling when I walked into his office. Well, that was a first.

His lawyer was in the corner, looking put-upon as usual. There was no doubt in my mind that he objected to every part of this plan - but he was objecting all the way to the bank, it seemed. I knew how he felt.

"Good morning, Maddy. Please, have a seat." He gestured to a chair that was facing his desk.

There was a rather nice fountain pen sitting conspicuously on the polished wood, waiting for me. I sat down and picked it up. It could have been a fifty dollar pen or a five thousand dollar pen - what was the difference, really? - but considering its owner, I had a pretty good idea which one was more likely.

"You like it?" Daniel wanted to know, noticing me studying the pen. I looked up, startled.

"Uh, yeah," I said. "I...yeah, I do." Really, I had been focusing on absolutely anything except the reality of what I was about to do, but sure, the pen was nice.

"Keep it," he said. "It's yours."

"Oh, no, I couldn't. I'll lose it."

"What's mine is yours, Maddy. You'd better get used to that idea."

I swallowed with difficulty. I felt like my throat was closing up, but I forced myself to take a deep breath as he pushed a series of papers towards me and pointed to the spots where I was meant to sign. He signed after me, with an elegant flourish, and then handed the whole thing over to his lawyer.

"Thank you," he said, reaching across the desk to shake my hand. Which seemed like an odd gesture, considering the intimacy of our arrangement, but I took it. "You won't regret your decision, I promise."

"You can't possibly promise that," I replied, smiling. "But you're welcome."

I was useless for the rest of the day, flitting from project to project and accomplishing nothing. I could tell that Florence noticed, but she managed to restrain herself from commenting on it until after lunch.

"What's up with you? You look like you're a million miles away."

"I'm fine," I replied quickly. Too quickly. My ears were burning. Good. "Just feeling a little under the weather today, I guess."

"Sure," said Florence. She wasn't convinced, which was fine by me. I tried to imagine her knowing smile when the news "got out." Ugh. Somehow, it hadn't occurred to me until now that I was going to have to endure inane congratulations from everyone in the office - about half of which, I knew, would be coming through gritted teeth. Every woman in the company carried at least a little torch for Daniel, if only because of his bank account. Oh God, what if they wanted to throw me an engagement party? I didn't think I could handle hours of their eyes staring into me like daggers, and their faces contorting into forced smiles every time I looked at them. There was so much about this arrangement that I hadn't even considered. How was I going to tell my parents? *Was* I going to tell my parents?

I sighed. My relationship with my parents was complicated. I preferred not to think about it too much, but this situation was forcing me to consider things I'd been ignoring for a long time. Like - who was I going to invite to the wedding? Or would we just have a small ceremony at City Hall? He probably wanted to get things over with as quickly as possible. Which was fine with me, as long as he provided the witnesses. Aside from my casual acquaintances at work, I hadn't really made any friends since I'd moved here. All of my close friends from college and high school were off living their own lives, and aside from the occasional online chat, I never spoke to them anymore.

My head was swimming when I climbed into the town car at the end of the day, and I barely answered the driver when he spoke to me. Realistically, I knew Daniel would help me figure out a way to deal with any issues that came up. He was highly motivated to ensure the success of our little scheme. But I was still going to worry.

I felt like a zombie for the rest of the night, but of course I couldn't sleep when I finally crawled into bed. When I finally drifted off to sleep, it happened so gradually that I shifted seamlessly from meandering thoughts into a dream.

I was thinking about Daniel, naturally, imagining a conversation we'd have in his office when we next met. But as my brain slowly drifted from sleeping to waking, there was an almost-imperceptible shift in the feeling of the room. I could feel that something was about to happen - something important. He stood up and walked out from behind his desk, coming towards me. I thought he was speaking - something about my "marital duties," with a wicked smile on his face. Every nerve in my body was tingling with anticipation by the time he touched me. His fingers burned a trail down the side of my face, to my neck, to my chest, and suddenly I was laid out on the top of his desk with my blouse unbuttoned and my skirt riding up my thighs.

This being a dream - which I knew somehow, even as I sighed and parted my legs for him - he knew exactly how to touch me, knew all of the secret places that made me shudder and bite my lip. I could feel my nipples pucker and tighten as two of his fingers travelled down the valley between my breasts, pausing to dip into my navel before sliding down my lower stomach and stopping, teasingly, just above my mound.

He smiled.

He leaned over me, resting his elbow on the desk and brushing his lips against mine - an almost-but-not-quite kiss. I could feel my face burning, my chest heaving with every breath; I'd completely fallen to pieces and he'd hardly touched me at all. Yet.

The part of my brain that was aware I was dreaming drifted further and further away, allowing me to lose myself in the fantasy. No one in real life, not even Daniel himself, could possibly live up to this. But I might as well enjoy it while it lasted.

I arched my back, signaling that I was more than ready for him. Then and only then, he grabbed me by the hips and pulled me to the edge of the desk, pulling my legs apart further until my skirt was bunched up around my waist. He leaned down and pressed a burning kiss on the inside of my thigh -

Bzzt! Bzzt! Bzzt! Bzzt!

My arm flailed vaguely in the direction of my bedside table, grasping for my vibrating phone, my spastic movements sending it flying across the room. It sat on the carpet, still buzzing away, until I dragged myself out from under the covers to shut the alarm up.

Oh, God. How was I going to look Daniel in the eye now?

Chapter Three

The memory of the dream was still vivid in the back of my mind as I walked through the doors into the office. I kept my head down, hurrying to my desk to settle in before anyone tried to strike up a conversation with me. And God forbid I should run into Daniel. Come to think of it, though, I'd never actually witnessed him coming or going. As far as I knew, he slept here.

Okay, no, that wasn't the ideal way to take my mind off of my dream. I forced myself to focus on the work that was on my screen, blocking out any thoughts or feelings that weren't directly related to this booklet design. It didn't have a firm deadline, so I'd been tinkering around with it for weeks. I wondered what would happen to it, after I "quit." As mind-numbing as my work could sometimes be, I still took a tiny bit of creative pride in what I did for the company. It felt strange to know that I'd be saying goodbye to all of that.

"Maddy."

I felt a hot flush spread across the back of my neck at the sound of his voice. Turning around slowly, I forced myself to meet his gaze. He was standing there casually, like it was the most natural thing in the world, his arm resting on the top of the cubicle wall.

"Good morning, sir," I said. Everyone in

neighborhood cubicles had slowly rotated their chairs around to stare at us, and anyone passing through the vicinity had stopped a little distance away, pretending to be interested in a yellowed newspaper cartoon pinned to someone's wall while they listened to our conversation.

I knew this was exactly what Daniel wanted, but I still couldn't stop myself from blushing. "I'm glad to see you here so early," he said. "Do you have any plans for lunch today?"

I swallowed hard and shook my head.

"Excellent," he said. "I hope you'll join me in my office at eleven-thirty. We'll order in. Whatever you like. I want to discuss some new ideas I have about the project."

"Of course," I said, a little louder than necessary. "I'll see you then."

"Very good." He nodded, smiled, hesitated for a moment, and then walked away. Everyone's eyes followed him until he disappeared behind his office door, and then they all turned to me.

I hunched over my keyboard, pretending I couldn't feel their eyes drilling holes in my back. I spent the next half hour nudging the same block of text back and forth, and when I finally looked up, everyone had returned to their rightful places. But I knew what they were thinking.

Now, I had to spend my whole lunch break

sitting across the desk from him. How was I going to avoid blushing and giggling the whole time? Or worse, just staring at him like a deer in the headlights? I hated being reduced to an airheaded schoolgirl by one stupid dream, but it felt so real.

The next few hours flew by. Before long, I found myself walking down the thickly carpeted hallway that led to Daniel's office. His door was open a crack, and his assistant was standing by his desk with a notepad open.

"Ah, Ms. Wainright," he said, gesturing for me to sit. "I was just about to give Alice my lunch order. I was thinking of takeout from Vivian's - how does that sound?"

"Great, it sounds great," I replied, after I managed to find my voice. Vivian's was one of the most expensive steak houses in town. I'd never dreamed of setting foot in the place. But to Daniel, it was probably like going to a sub shop for lunch. No big deal. This lifestyle was going to take some adjusting-to.

"Alice, I'll have a twelve-ounce Porterhouse with mashed potatoes and grilled asparagus. Medium rare. Ms. Wainright, what about you?"

"Oh, I don't really...I don't really know what they have." Daniel and Alice were both staring at me expectantly, and I felt like I was being tested somehow.

"All the usual," said Daniel, waving his hand

vaguely. "They'll make you anything. What do you like, steak? Chicken? Seafood? I think I've had everything there at least once, I could recommend you something."

"I'm not picky," I said, truthfully. "I was going to have mostly-smashed energy bar from the bottom of my purse, so pretty much anything would be a step up from that."

Daniel laughed, but Alice shot me a haughty look. "Would you rather have something light, then?" said Daniel. "A salad, maybe? Their Caesar with grilled shrimp is really excellent; the dressing is a special in-house recipe."

"Sure, that sounds fantastic." I cleared my throat as Alice hurried out of the room with her notepad. "Do you get lunch at Vivian's often?"

"Just a few times a week." He was smiling at me, knowingly. "I promise you, my life isn't all that strange. You'll get used to it. Which brings me to my next point - I feel we ought to go out on our first official dinner date sooner rather than later. I'm sure the office gossip mill is going to start soon."

"My cube-mate asked me yesterday why I was spending so much time in your office," I supplied, trying not to fidget in my seat. But I couldn't stop myself from staring at his lips, trying to remember if the recreation from my dream was accurate to real life. I could feel a prickling heat travel up the skin on my chest as my eyes travelled along the sleek, polished surface of his desk, remembering how it had "felt" under my body. Almost subconsciously, I had worn a knee-length skirt and blouse very similar to the outfit my brain had conjured up. I still couldn't really explain why. Did I think it was going to make him notice me? Did I *want* him to notice me?

The last thing I needed was to harbor a one-sided crush on my fake husband.

"Is it going to be somewhere fancy?" I blurted out, trying to disrupt my very dangerous thought patterns. He blinked at me. "I mean, the dinner date. I don't really think I have anything to wear."

"Yes, I was about to ask..." he dug out his wallet and pulled out a crisp off-white business card, handing it to me across the desk. "If you go to this boutique, you should find the staff very accommodating. They have my credit card on file. I'll call ahead and let them know to expect you. Buy whatever you like. Don't hold yourself back; you'll certainly find occasion to wear all of it in the next year."

I stared at the card. "Thank you."

He steered the conversation to small talk for the next few minutes, covering everything from the unseasonably warm weather to a funny news article he'd seen that morning. I'd never known him to be this talkative, or this casual, and I found myself growing quieter and quieter. I was still trying to digest the strangeness of it all; trying to picture myself walking into the boutique. I felt like the mere act of shopping there required nicer clothes than I had in my closet.

Alice returned with our food in record time. Daniel was right. The salad was delicious, but I could barely taste it. My eyes kept drifting to his mouth, watching the way it closed around each bite, the way his tongue flicked out to lick his lips clean -

Okay, I had a serious problem on my hands. I just had to hope it would wear off once the memory of the dream faded. Because if this was permanent, the next year of my life was going to be an elaborate form of torture.

I was relieved to escape from his office, hurrying back to my desk. I buried myself in meaningless busy work for the rest of the day. I survived the rest of the week that way, and to my surprise, I fielded exactly zero questions about the nature of my relationship with Daniel. I really expected someone to say something; a few times I swore someone was about to, but then they clammed up and retreated. Maybe Daniel intimidated them. He certainly did me. Being perfectly honest with myself, I was terrified of disappointing him in some way. He obviously thought I was more than capable of pretending to be his wife for legal purposes, but I had my doubts. What if I made some terrible blunder, or revealed something incriminating to the INS? What if I just did something horribly embarrassing - something that would force him to stand up for me as if I were really his wife?

I went to the boutique on Saturday, slipping into the newest jeans I had and a pretty decent blouse that didn't have a single stain on it. Still, the moment the bell jingled above my head as I walked through the door, I was painfully aware of being out of my element. I ought to have worn high heels, or gotten my hair done, or *something*. One of the sales girls came over to me, and I felt like her smile was a little bit forced.

"Can I help you?" she asked, looking me up and down.

"I need a dress," I said. "I'm sure you can tell I'm out of my element. Daniel Thorne told me to come here, he said -"

"Oh, of *course*." Her demeanor instantly thawed. "Right over here, Ms. Wainright. It's a pleasure to meet you. My name's Emma. I've pulled a few pieces for you. Let me know what you think. Mr. Thorne wasn't sure of your size, but I'm sure we can find it if you like any of them."

"To be perfectly honest, I'm not sure I know my size either. It's been so long since I've bought a dress." I looked up at what she'd chosen for me; there was something black and slinky and something else in a deep purple, and more behind those that I couldn't really see.

"Let's take your measurements, then. Step into a fitting room." She was already unwinding a tailor's tape.

Once she'd wrapped it around my waist, hips, and bust, she scribbled a few things on a notepad I hadn't even noticed she had. "All right," she said. "A few of these will probably fit you just fine, but we can work with the others as well. Why don't you try the black one on first?"

I stepped out of my clothes and slipped it over my head, spinning around in the mirror as the folds of fabric settled on the curves and contours of my body. I had to admit I liked the way it clung to my chest, but I wasn't happy with the overall shape of it. I looked to Emma for guidance.

She shook her head. "It's not quite right for you. I had a feeling it wouldn't be. Try the purple."

Close, but it still didn't look right to me. Then again, I wasn't sure if my expectations of how I would look in a dress were very realistic. I was thinking of magazine photo shoots airbrushed all to hell. No matter what I wore, I was still going to have all the lumps and bumps of a real human woman.

Emma was tugging at the hem. It fell at an odd place, just below my knee, which threw off the whole look of the dress.

"We can take this in a little bit, if you end up liking it," she said. "But let's try something else. I think Mr. Thorne wants you to have something off the rack. He made it sound like time was a factor, and I've got a few clients ahead of you in line for alterations."

I nodded, and she dug through her selections for a moment, finally pulling out something in the deepest shade of midnight blue I'd ever seen. Instantly, the color transported me back to a fond childhood memory of walking through the mall, hand-in-hand with my mom, before things went sour between us. I'd look up at the massive skylights that lined the main concourses, just after dusk, seeing the sky just as it turned this particular shade of blue. I couldn't explain why, but something about that color always made my young heart swell with the beauty of it.

Emma was smiling. "Here," she said. "I can tell you're in love with it already. Try it on."

It was light and silky, fitting over me like a second skin, but not clinging too tight. My breath caught in my throat as I looked at my reflection. Almost instinctively, I reached up and undid my ponytail, letting my hair fall loose around my shoulders. I tossed my head. *Now* I looked like someone who belonged on Daniel's arm.

Emma's smile had broken into a grin, lighting her whole face up with the satisfaction of a job well done. I felt a scratch against my armpit, and I remembered for the first time that these dresses had price tags. But as I lifted my arm and tried to grab onto the tag with my other hand, Emma stepped forward and gently pulled my hand away.

"I'm sorry, but I'm under very particular instructions not to let you look at the price."

I stared at her. "Are you serious?"

She smiled. "Come on. Let's find you some accessories."

Emma showed me a necklace and a pair of earrings, elegant silver pieces with alternating light blue and white pearls and crystal pendants, far more delicate and beautiful than anything I'd ever worn. She put me in front of a mirror and fastened the necklace while I slipped the earrings in.

It was perfect. The lighter blue of the jewelry was beautifully complemented by the midnight blue of the fabric, and when Emma pulled my hair into a quick bun on the top of my head, I hardly even recognized myself. A pair of matching shoes, and I looked ready for the red carpet.

Walking out of the shop, I tried not to even think about how much money I'd just spent. Daniel wanted me to have these things. That was the important part. A few hundred - or, God forbid, a few *thousand* dollars were nothing to him in exchange for me having a nice outfit.

My phone went off just as I walked through the door of my apartment. Sighing, I dropped my purchases on the couch and dug it out of my purse. Unknown Name, Unknown Number. I almost let it go to voicemail, but changed by mind at the last minute.

"Hello?"

"Hello, Maddy. How are you?"

"Daniel." I stopped in the middle of my living room, my heart thudding at the sound of his voice. I'd really been looking forward to a whole weekend of being away from him, avoiding his knowing smiles and deep green eyes and all the things that reminded me of that damn dream. "I just got back from the boutique, actually."

"Oh, did Emma treat you well?"

"Yeah, once I dropped your name." I switched the phone to my other ear and picked up the bag, pulling the necklace and earrings out. "She set me up pretty well."

"Glad to hear it. I'm sorry if she was cold to you at first. They've had issues with 'customers' who come in without the intention of buying anything, just putting on a little fashion show for themselves and making a mess in their wake."

"And I looked like one of *those* people. Yeah, I get it."

Daniel was silent for a moment, as if he wasn't quite sure if I was being snarky or not.

"I wanted to ask you if you were free for dinner tonight," he said, finally.

"Already?" I set the jewelry down. "I thought you meant, like...next week, or something."

"I've been thinking about it since, and I feel it would be best to get things off the ground soon. If you're free, of course."

It was on the tip of my tongue to say something bitingly sarcastic, but instead, I just said "of course."

"I'll send a car to pick you up at seven o'clock."

"Sure," I said, hanging up before he had a chance to say goodbye.

I couldn't explain why I was so irritated. Something about Emma's demeanor, and his explanation for it, was more than I could stomach. I didn't want to spend the next year pretending to be something I wasn't, just to fit in. But I'd already signed the contract.

I sat down heavily on the couch, picking up the sparkling necklace and toying with it gently. Could I get used to this lifestyle? Did I even *want* to?

I busied myself around the apartment for the rest of the day, vacuuming and dusting and wiping down corners I hadn't touched since I moved in. My eyes kept drifting over to the bag from the boutique, and I couldn't stop myself from thinking about everything that it symbolized. Years of financial freedom. More money than I had ever dreamed of. A new lifestyle. A new *life*.

When the car pulled up, I was waiting outside, clutching my new black leather purse and trying not to look awkward.

"Forgive me, ma'am, but you look lovely," said the driver as I climbed in. I had to smile.

"Thank you," I replied. "Let's hope Daniel agrees."

The driver cleared his throat, and I could tell he wanted to say something.

"What?" I prompted, finally.

"Well, I shouldn't say anything, but..." He met my eyes in the rear view. "I've been suspecting there was something going on between you two."

Been suspecting? How long had the driver even been aware of my existence? I felt a chill run up my spine, but I was afraid to ask the question.

"Well, you've got solid instincts," I said. "Where are we going, by the way?"

"The Inn at Grenarnia," he replied, in a tone of voice that suggested he'd never set foot in that restaurant himself. I felt like I wanted to scream. I knew the place - they'd been written up in the paper before, with words of high praise for their $250-a-plate tasting menus. How on earth was I supposed to behave naturally in a place like that?

"Wow," I managed, after a silence. "Fancy."

"Well, that's how Daniel is when he really likes someone. No expense spared. He must really want to impress you."

Or intimidate me. "I guess so," I said.

He'd pulled up to the curb in front of the restaurant. I took a deep breath, smoothed my dress over my thighs, and stepped out onto the sidewalk.

Chapter Four

I had to admit, the restaurant was enchanting. And I hadn't even set foot inside the door yet. They had a large veranda where couples sat on swings and Adirondack chairs, talking, laughing and sipping wine. Strings of lights twinkled like fireflies all around the eaves. Off to the side, there was a lush garden, and as I stepped closer to get a better look, Daniel walked out from under the ivy-covered trellis.

"Maddy," he said, warmly, coming towards me and taking my hand. He held it for a moment, and I had the strange thought that he was going to lift it to his lips. Instead, he simply squeezed it a little before letting go. "That's a stunning dress, by the way."

"Hi," I said. "This, uh, this place is really nice."

"It's cute, isn't it?"

That wasn't exactly the word I would have chosen for a place that cost this much, but I just nodded and smiled.

There was a table waiting for us inside, surrounded by glowing candles and plants that seemed to be growing out of the floor. On closer inspection, they proved to be thriving in planter boxes that were built in to be at the same level. In the center of the dining room, there was a massive tree trunk; the restaurant appeared to have been built around it.

"You look surprised," Daniel said, smiling.

"I wasn't really expecting it to be like this," I said. "I don't know what I was expecting."

"I can't stand a stuffy restaurant," he said. "As far as I'm concerned, it's not 'nice' if you can't be comfortable while you're there."

We had a reservation for the tasting menu - of *course* - which was actually somewhat of a relief. At least I didn't have to try and choose the entrée that would make me stand out the least as someone who didn't belong there.

But as time went on, I was plagued less and less with the feeling of sticking out like a sore thumb. By the time the server cleared away our third set of plates, each with a tiny Angus rib eye fillet on a bed of roasted potatoes and red wine-marinated onions, I was talking and laughing like anything. I was just finishing up my second glass of wine, and I was beginning to feel the pleasant, heady buzz. Slowly but surely, I was becoming less aware of everyone in the room except for me and Daniel.

"You didn't have to bring me here, you know," I heard myself blurting out in the middle of an unrelated conversation. Oh, God. Why on earth had I let those words slip out? That wasn't what I meant to say at all.

But Daniel just laughed. He was beginning to feel it a little himself, I could tell; his eyes were brighter, the skin of his cheeks rosier, than I'd ever seen. Even in the low light, his transformation from businessman to just *man* was very noticeable.

"Yes I did," he replied, easily.

"No, I mean..." I leaned over the table, consciously lowering my voice a little. "We could have just *said* we went."

"Trust me," Daniel countered, his face growing serious again. "In the circles I run, it's best to back up your claims with as many facts as possible. The staff here all knows the same people I do; they bring all their first dates here. By being seen here with you tonight, I'm establishing my backstory." He smiled, suddenly. "And having a pretty good time, wouldn't you agree?"

I nodded, crashing back to earth with the sudden reminder of why we were really here.

"I'm sorry," I said. "I didn't mean to…bring that up right now. I just, I didn't want to get too carried away."

If he wondered what I meant by that, he didn't ask, thank God. *I* wasn't even sure what I meant by that. I hadn't intended to let on that I was already starting to lose perspective on our "relationship." I was sure the last thing he wanted was for me to actually fall for him. It would make everything so complicated. Why did my brain always have to do things like this? Why did it have to be so stupid?

"I understand," he said. "Don't worry. If you ever have any questions or concerns about how I'm choosing to handle all of…this," he made a vague gesture, "please don't hesitate to ask."

"Sure," I said, reaching for my refilled wine glass and taking a substantial swallow.

Daniel sat back in his chair, rearranging his face into the mask of a man who was having a great time on a first date. I cursed silently. Even

I'd been taken in for a while there. Of course he was just pretending.

We were at the dessert courses by now, and I could hardly taste the tiny, re-imagined tiramisu that I shoved into my mouth. All I could do at this point was pray that things got less awkward the more time we spent together.

Or, not. I could put up with a year of awkwardness for two million dollars, couldn't I? Hell, I'd been putting up with a lifetime of awkwardness all on my own. And I had no one but myself to blame for that.

"So, Maddy," Daniel said, gently rolling the stem of his empty wineglass between his thumb and forefinger, rotating the glass a half-turn, over and over again. "What were you doing with yourself before you came to work for me?"

His words were positively dripping with meaning. Was this how he talked to people he was actually trying to seduce? Did it even occur to him, that while the sensible part of my mind understood he was faking, he was still going to make my hormones rage?

He sounded exactly like in my dream.

I had to forget about that fucking *dream*.

I cleared my throat, trying to ignore the sound of my heart pounding in my ears. "Retail," I said, simply. "And college before that."

"Where do you go to school?"

"The Institute, downtown."

"For graphic design?"

I nodded.

"You're very talented, you know," he said.

I looked around me instinctively, as if he could be talking to someone else.

"Thank you," I said, finally. My voice sounded very far away. I reached for my water glass. The ice was all melted, bringing the level of the water up high enough to slosh some on myself as I took a drink. I groaned, reaching for a napkin to dab myself off.

I'd really done it. I'd managed to get uncoordinated-drunk on my first date with a billionaire. *Great job, Maddy!*

Daniel chuckled, his eyes sparkling. "No more wine tonight, maybe," he said. "Would you like some coffee?"

"Coffee doesn't sober you up," I muttered. "That's a myth."

"I know," he said. "But would you like some anyway?"

"Sure. Fine." I dragged myself into a more proper posture in my chair. "Can I ask *you* some questions, Daniel?"

"Anything."

"Everybody says you're a billionaire, is that true?"

His eyes scanned the table. He actually looked a little uncomfortable, but I must have been mistaken about that.

"I suppose," he said. "I'm not Bill Gates or anything like that."

"No," I replied, unable to stop the lopsided grin that spread across my face. "No, you're certainly not."

He looked up again and smiled back, a little...*bashfully*?

"I live comfortably," he said. "I've never tried to hide that."

"Sorry." In retrospect, I didn't know what came over me. I knew it was rude to ask people about money. For some reason, the fact that he was so freakishly rich made me feel like the rules didn't apply in this situation. But no matter how much money the guy had, he probably didn't want to feel like he was being stared at in the zoo. I realized I was blushing.

"It's all right," he said. "I can certainly understand the curiosity. And I did say you could ask me anything. To be perfectly honest, I don't really know much money I have at the moment. That sounds appalling. Doesn't it? God." He laughed a little, sounding bewildered at himself. "But it doesn't really feel like mine. Most of it came from investments my father set up for me when I was a teenager. I never really see it. I feel like you're about to burst out laughing at me."

"I'm sorry," I said. I *was* tittering. "It's

just...the fact that you can have all this money and not even touch it. I can't even imagine. You know?"

"I do. Believe it or not, it wasn't always like this for me."

He sipped his water, and something in his face told me this was the end of that discussion, for now.

I lowered my voice. "Do your parents know about your...plan?"

He hesitated for a moment. "They've both passed," he said, finally, looking up from the table.

"Oh. I'm sorry." I felt like I was doing nothing but apologizing tonight.

He shrugged. "The fewer people know about it, the better. We can talk about this later, if you like. I'd rather not continue this conversation in public."

"Of course."

Well, this was going fantastic. If this were a real first date, I would have blown it completely. I hunched over the table, staring down into the steaming cup of organic free trade gourmet roasted coffee that I hadn't touched. Daniel was waving the server down for the check.

Once he'd filled it out with his own elegant pen, produced from an inner jacket pocket, he leaned over the table again and spoke in soft murmur.

"I think it's best, for appearance's sake, if we leave in the same car. And I would appreciate it very much if you would come home with me and spend the night."

My throat tightened. "So soon?"

"Well, by this time, we've been having an affair for a few weeks now. It only makes sense you would come home with me after our 'first date,' if only because it's hardly our first *date*."

"Fine," I said.

He was almost whispering now. "You can stay in your own room." He smiled. "With a lock on the door. I have no plans to take advantage of you. Right now, everyone here thinks I'm telling you about all the naughty things I'm going to do to you, when we get back. Smile back. *Smile back*."

I did, even as goose bumps rose all over my skin. "It's a good thing the acoustics are so bad in here," I purred, slipping my foot out of my shoe and resting it lightly on top of his. It was dark, but the tablecloths were certainly short enough that someone might see, if they happened to look. His eyebrows went up a fraction of an inch. I wasn't sure if it was the situation, or the man, or the wine, or some combination of all three, but I felt bold.

"I hope their imaginations are sufficiently filthy to put the right words in my mouth," I said, slowly stroking the small part of his leg I could reach with my toe under the cuff of his pants. It was the first time we'd touched, other than shaking hands. I could feel his eyes on me - and the eyes of a few other patrons as well - but I refused to look up, instead pouring a little cream into my coffee, stirring it, and then raising the spoon to my mouth. I slid it into my mouth and licked it clean with an exaggerated gesture. It would be laughable under normal circumstances, but I hoped the alcohol and the atmosphere would work in my favor. If I could at least make Daniel half as uncomfortable as he was making me, then I would win.

Of course, it was backfiring horribly as well. I couldn't tell if the look on his face was entirely acting or not, but I was tingling all over. Even through my pantyhose and the fabric of his sock, I could feel the heat of his skin on my foot. Suddenly, my mouth was very dry.

In the low light, his eyes looked dark. It was impossible to tell if his pupils had really grown large, or if perhaps something else was growing -

No, no no. *Snap out of it, Maddy!*

I pulled my foot away abruptly, clearing my throat and straightening up in my chair. The spell was broken.

His car arrived a few minutes later, and I let him lift me to my feet and lead me outside, his hand resting on the small of my back. Yes. There it was. And so soon, too.

Later on, our relationship would be described as "whirlwind." I was sure of it.

He had a place downtown, at one of those high-rise buildings with a doorman. An actual doorman. In this day and age. I caught his eye and nodded, tittering and leaning on Daniel's arm. Playing just slightly more drunk than I really was. The doorman nodded and favored me with a knowing smile.

The elevator ride seemed to take ages. A heavy silence permeated the car. I ran my fingers through my hair, my head still buzzing with the wine and the thrill of deception. The doorman thought we were an item. *Everyone* was going to think we were an item. There was a certain perverse joy in the whole thing, I had to admit.

"What's so funny?" Daniel said, and I realized I was grinning like an idiot.

"I don't know," I said. "Just, everything."

He seemed slightly bothered as we finally reached our floor and stepped out into the hallway. I wasn't sure what I'd said or done to offend him. Then again, it could have been any single thing I'd done, or a combination of all my missteps finally come home to roost. What if he was regretting his decision to choose me? The thought made me feel sick to my stomach -

because of the money, I was almost sure. And of course I never liked disappointing anyone.

He unlocked the front door, and we both stepped inside.

The front of his apartment looked like a furniture showroom. My shoes clacked on the polished hardwood floors as I walked down the hall, past a little table made of sleek black wood, with a small live bamboo plant on top of it. It was situated as if it might be a place for the mail, except that putting the mail there would ruin the illusion of a perfect design magazine home. Deeper into the room, there were two spotless white couches sitting face-to-face on either side of a gray runner rug that led towards a massive fireplace. I stepped out of my shoes and sighed, resisting the urge to rub my temples.

"I'll be back in a moment," said Daniel, heading towards the loft staircase that I assumed led to his bedroom. "Make yourself at home."

I collapsed on one of the sofas, slumping in a very unladylike fashion not befitting of my elegant apparel. The ceiling looked like it was a thousand miles away. I shivered a little, hugging my bare arms. Excessively high ceilings always made me feel cold, for some reason.

Daniel came back down the stairs two at a time, his tie gone, shirt un-tucked, and sleeves rolled up to the elbows. "Can I get you something?"

I shook my head. "I think I'd just like to go to bed."

He hesitated for a moment. "Of course. Tomorrow, if you don't have other plans, I was hoping you could stay over and work on our story for the INS interviews."

"Sure," I said, getting to my feet. "Which way?"

"You can have your pick of the two guest rooms. Here, I'll show you."

He walked ahead of me down the hallway, opening the first door we encountered. "Here's the bathroom. I've put out some fresh towels." He moved on to the next door, pushing it open and flicking on the light. "This is the main guest room."

I peeked in. It was every bit as sterile and un-lived-in as the rest of the apartment. "Okay," I said.

"And here's the other. It's a bit smaller, but some people prefer that."

I followed him further down the hall.

At least this one looked a little bit like a normal bedroom. It was cozy, just the right size, and there wasn't a bamboo plant in sight. "Yeah, this'll work."

"I had a feeling you'd pick this one. There are some fresh clothes in the closet; Emma gave me some guidance on that."

"Thanks," I said. I could have sworn that my brain was telling my feet to walk forward, to go into the room and shut the door. But I just kept standing in the doorway, inches from Daniel, hyper-aware of the sound of his breathing.

"You really do look stunning in that dress," he said. "I wasn't just saying that."

I swallowed before I spoke. "That's not what you said before."

"It's not?"

"No, you just said 'stunning dress.'"

"Well, I meant *you* look stunning. The dress just complements it."

My eyes drifted to the floor, instinctively. Accepting complements gracefully was not among my talents. "That's very nice of you to say," I muttered.

"Look at me," he said, his voice soft and persuasive.

I did. He looked as if he were struggling to say something, or perhaps struggling not to say it.

"Hey," I said. "I'm really tired. We can talk tomorrow, okay?"

"Yes," he said, finally. "Of course. I'm sorry. Good night, Maddy."

He withdrew abruptly, and was gone in a moment. I shut myself in my room and flopped over onto the bed, trying not to let myself think too hard about what had just happened between us. For the first time, I was sure I'd seen Daniel's façade crack. I was *sure* he had some genuine attraction for me, beyond what he was required to display for the sake of our "relationship."

Then again, maybe he'd just been swept up in the seductive atmosphere of the evening. Hell, maybe *he'd* had a sex dream about *me*.

I sat up, biting my lip. It had been a joke in my own head, but the idea of weighing so heavily in his thoughts that he couldn't even escape me in his dreams...a powerful man rendered helpless, writhing between the sheets, wanting me, needing me...

No, no, *no*. I had to keep my head screwed on straight. These weren't harmless fantasies; not when I was going to be living with his man and pretending to be his wife. I was going to lose sight of what we were really doing. I was going to fall for him if I wasn't careful.

There it was. That was the first time I'd really admitted it to myself, in as many words. Was I really that pathetic, to fall in love with a man simply because he was creating a believable facsimile of wooing me? Admittedly, he was good at it. The dress, the restaurant, the way he'd looked at me, like I was the only thing in the world he'd ever wanted. It was enough to turn anyone's head around.

I was pretty sure I remembered reading somewhere - or maybe learning in a class - about how a large percentage of humans' affection for each other is purely related to proximity.

"Well, I'm fucked," I said out loud to the empty room.

Chapter Five

I wasn't sure if it was the sunlight or the noises from the kitchen that woke me up. I dragged myself out of bed and down the hallway to the bathroom with some difficulty; I'd finally been able to drift off to sleep after hours of staring at the ceiling in the dark, but I definitely hadn't gotten any decent rest.

After a quick shower, I felt slightly more human. I wrapped up in a thick, fluffy robe and padded down the hallway towards the kitchen. Daniel turned around when he heard one of the stools at the elegant breakfast bar scraping along the floor.

He was wearing jeans and a tee shirt that said something about a corporate fun run in 2008. So he *did* know how to dress like a normal person. That was encouraging.

I just wished the sight of it didn't make my

mouth water.

Well, maybe I was just hungry.

"Good morning," he said, smiling at me. His eyes flicked up and down a few times, as if he hadn't expected me to come to breakfast in a bathrobe. But what the hell - we were going to be married soon, right?

"Hi," I said. His hair was falling loose over his forehead, and I couldn't stop staring at it, wanting to push it back into its proper place. "I like your...shirt."

I'd almost said pants. Clearly, I just needed to keep my mouth shut.

"Thank you," he said, taking it as gracefully as anyone might be expected to. "How do you take your eggs?"

"Over medium, I guess." I couldn't remember the last time I'd eaten eggs that I didn't prepare for myself. As it turned out, he made them just the way I liked - gooey but not runny, no uncooked whites. While I dipped my toast in the yolk, I watched him eat the frittata he'd made for himself. There was a veritable rainbow of chopped vegetables mixed in, almost more than there were eggs. No toast. So this was how he maintained his figure. For some reason, I'd always imagined him as one of those people who can eat absolutely anything and never gain an ounce. It was comforting to know he had a human side after all.

After breakfast, I got dressed in the surprisingly casual clothes he'd picked for me, and we settled down in the living room. Daniel pulled out a small notepad and pen.

"We need to get our story straight on certain details of our relationship," he said. "Since we'll be living together, and acting as a couple, we ought to be able to give genuine answers to most of the questions. But there will be questions about the beginning of our relationship, about very personal things we might not know about each other. They'll be the sorts of questions that are difficult to fake. When it comes to the time of the interview, if they ask you a difficult question that we haven't prepared for, simply say that you don't know or you can't remember the details of what they're asking about. Never try to guess or make up an answer."

I nodded. Just the thought of the interview was already making me nervous, even though it was likely to be months and months away.

"You'll probably be expected to describe the features, layout, and décor of this place," he said. "But that shouldn't be too difficult after a while. When it comes to those sorts of questions, make sure to be accurate, but not too thorough. You don't want to sound rehearsed."

"Jesus," I said, more to myself than him.

He looked up, mildly startled. "You're not

having second thoughts, are you?"

"No, no." I played with the hem of my new shirt. "It's just...it's a lot, is all."

"You'll do fine." He touched my shoulder, rested his hand there for a moment, and then pulled it away abruptly. His eyes flicked back down to his notepad. "Your birthday...May 16th, 1986. Yes?"

I nodded.

"Mine is November 7th, 1982. Memorize it." He turned the page. "What were some of the first things we talked about, when our relationship became personal? What did we have in common?"

"Are you asking me to make something up right now?"

"If we discuss these things, we'll both be more likely to remember."

"All right, so...Woody Allen movies?"

He blinked. "Sorry?"

"That's what we had in common. We both liked Woody Allen movies and we started talking about it."

His brow was just slightly furrowed.

I sighed. "Fine, what's your idea, then?"

"I don't know."

"But you don't like mine."

"It just...sounds made up."

"Those are some awfully judgmental words coming from a man with no ideas."

"Fine." He scribbled on the notepad. "We'll put it down as a temporary answer and we can revise it later if I think of something better."

"I don't think that's a good idea. If we keep changing things, we're going to get confused. We need to pick something and stick with it. Don't you think?"

He exhaled. "All right. We both liked Woody Allen. What about our first meeting? Can you describe it?"

"In real life, or are we coming up with an alternate reality for this too?"

"In real life. Everyone knows you work for me, so that's obviously when we met."

I crossed my arms, thinking. "I'm not sure we ever really did 'meet.' I saw you, obviously. But I don't know if we were ever formally introduced until you called me into your office to…discuss the special project."

"About that." He cleared this throat. "You found out later that there was, in fact, no special project. I only called you into my office because I wanted to talk to you. I'd become smitten from a distance. I wanted an excuse to have a conversation with you, and get to know you better. Or at all. That's when we discovered that we both liked Woody Allen. Over the next few days, I kept calling you to my office for more 'meetings.' Things became…physical, very quickly. We both kept it a secret, due to the conflict of interest. But then, I finally decided I didn't want to keep our love hidden anymore. So I asked you out to dinner with me. Shortly after that, you quit your job and moved into my apartment." He looked up, smiling slightly. "So, that's the story of us."

"Your alternate universe doppelganger is very aggressive," I said. "Did I have any say in the matter at all?"

He looked mildly offended. "Of course," he said. "What kind of fictional man do you think I am?"

I had to laugh. "All right, okay. What if they ask me if I knew about your...you know, predicament?"

"Of course I told you, because I didn't want you to think I was only marrying you for that. You were skeptical at first, of course, but as time went on, you realized that I genuinely loved you."

"That's very touching. Do you think they'll fall for it?"

"There's no law against marrying someone if you're at risk of being deported. What's illegal is marrying someone *because* you're at risk of being deported. It's all right for them to be suspicious that we might have rushed into things because of my situation, as long as they can't prove that was the only reason we got married."

"That sounds incredibly dodgy, just so you

know. If I worked for the INS I'd be driving you across the border myself."

"Your vote of confidence is much appreciated," he said dryly, flipping the page in his notebook. "But I told you, I have inside help. I have to go through the formalities, and I have to not trip over my own feet while doing so. They're even going to make a special exception for me. Normally, it would take two years of marriage before I could apply for a permanent visa, but they've reduced it to one."

"Thank God," I said out loud, without thinking.

He raised an eyebrow at me. "I realize you have no way of knowing this, but I promise being married to me won't be an actual nightmare."

I could feel my face turning bright red. "I know," I said, hastily. "I didn't mean...it's just, you know, a year of my life. That's scary enough to think about."

"Relax. I'm teasing you." He glanced down at his notepad again. "We need to pick a favorite sexual position."

I stared. "Is that a comment, or a question?"

"Just pick one," he said, still looking down at the paper.

"Uh, fine," I said. "Doggystyle? Is there like...a scientific term for that? Or something classier?"

"I don't think so," he muttered, scribbling something down.

"I hope you're actually writing down 'doggystyle' then," I said, willing myself to stop blushing furiously, even if there appeared to be no imminent danger of him raising his head.

I was wrong - he looked up at me then, frowning. "I'm not writing any of this down," he said, sharply. "And neither will you."

"Jesus." I raised both of my hands. "Do you see me taking notes?"

"I'm sorry." He toyed with his own pen for a moment. "I just...I can't emphasize how important it is that we don't have a written record of any of this. I'm taking notes that will help remind me of what we decide here, but no one else would be able to interpret them. Even so, I won't let this notebook out of my sight."

"I know," I said. "Believe me, I don't want to end up in prison for criminal conspiracy."

He chuckled. "Someone's been researching."

"I just wanted to know what the worst case scenario was. It's comforting."

"Let's not borrow trouble. It won't come to that if we're careful." He cleared his throat. "All right. They're very likely to ask about what kind of birth control we use, are you on anything I should know about?"

I shook my head. None of my relationships had lasted long enough for me to think about getting on anything long-term.

"Condoms, then," he said. "What kind?"

I snorted. "What *kind* of condoms?"

"That's exactly the kind of details they're going to ask about," he said, patiently. "Simple to answer if you're being honest, but very difficult if you're lying."

"Fine. I don't care. Whatever you normally use."

He hesitated. "Maybe it would be better if we said we were planning on having children as soon as possible."

"You don't think that's laying it on a little too thick?"

He was chewing on the side of his thumbnail. "Better they should think we're disgustingly in love, and wildly irresponsible, than faking it."

"Fine."

He flipped back through the pages of his notepad. "I think that's everything we need to go over. We'll review it from time to time. We shouldn't be called up for an interview until I submit some of my paperwork, but it's best to be prepared."

"Sure," I said.

He stood, tucking the notepad into his pocket. "Would you prefer to wait until after we're married to move in?"

I gaped at him for a moment before I spoke.

"Uh, yes. Please." I hadn't even considered that he might suggest otherwise, and the idea of sharing such close quarters with him gave me goose bumps. All right, so it was a big apartment. But it was still an apartment. An apartment where I'd shortly be living with him, for an entire year.

He looked slightly taken aback.

"I just need some more time," I said, quickly. "To get everything settled. You know. My lease - and everything."

He was frowning. "I'll pay it off," he said. "If that's a problem."

"I'm not ready," I said, a little more forcefully than I meant to. "If I have another problem that can be solved with money, trust me, you'll be the first to know."

Daniel stepped back. "Of course," he said, quietly. "I'm sorry."

I watched him as he disappeared up the staircase into his loft bedroom, leaving me alone on the sofa with my thoughts.

I felt vaguely sick to my stomach, sad and unsettled. I didn't like hurting his feelings, but he had to make more of an effort to understand how strange this whole situation was going to be for me. All that mattered to him was the end goal; with his eyes fixed on the prize, he seemed to be losing sight of the fact that he was asking me to give up my entire life.

The minutes ticked by, marked by the ultra-modern clock above the mantelpiece. Finally, I stood up and headed towards the staircase, because I didn't know what else to do.

The journey seemed to take forever, and I was acutely aware of the sound of every footfall. When I finally reached the top, I let my eyes drift over to the small sitting-area in the open part of the loft, two love seats facing each other with a little coffee table between. Finally I looked over to his bedroom door, which was hanging open.

He was sitting on the edge of a massive four-posted bed, so high off the floor that his feet dangled. He lifted his head when I walked in, and for the first time, I noticed the stress and exhaustion that was etched all over his face. Or maybe this was the first time he'd allowed me to see it.

I hoisted myself up on the mattress next to him.

"I'm sorry," I said. "But this is weird."

He nodded, sighing, as he dragged his fingers through his hair. Right now, he was a million miles away from the perfectly-groomed businessman I knew at work, the one whose hand I'd shaken to cement our strange agreement.

"I don't want to pressure you into anything that makes you uncomfortable," he said, finally.

"You know that, don't you? Just because I'm paying you...what I'm trying to say is, you shouldn't feel obligated."

"Okay," I said, laughing a little. I couldn't help it.

"What?"

"You know that's impossible, right?" I met his eyes. He genuinely didn't seem to understand what I was driving at. "With the amount of money you're giving me, how can I possibly *not* feel obligated?"

He shook his head. "You've got to stop thinking in those terms. I know it's...I know it's hard. The nature of what we're doing is so, so uh...if I thought there was another way, trust me, I'd do it. But we won't be able to pass as a genuine couple if we don't live as one. And because of that, I think things have the tendency to get...muddled."

He was struggling to find the right words. "It's like what we talked about before," I said. "About not letting things get too personal."

He shot me a tired smile. "But that's not really possible, is it? I think we're both learning that."

"Hey, I believe in us." I laid my hand on his shoulder, and felt his muscles tense under my hand. The gesture surprised even me, but at the same time, it felt right. "Here's to being as impersonal and robotic as possible while we pretend to be madly in love."

Daniel chuckled, and I pulled my hand away, slowly.

"I'm sure we can come out of this intact," I said. "We probably won't kill each other. Hey, maybe we'll even stay friends."

I hadn't meant for that to come out sounding so sincere. He looked away, a smile playing on his lips. "Why on earth would you want to be friends with me?" The question was addressed more to himself than it was to me, but I couldn't ignore it.

"What's that supposed to mean?" I prodded, jostling against him gently with my shoulder. I wasn't normally this into physical contact with near-strangers, but at this point I figured I might as well get used to touching him.

He was still looking at the carpet. "Maddy, if you ever need a favor, of course I'll help you. I don't expect a phone call on my birthday in exchange for that."

I didn't know what to say. This wasn't a side of him I'd ever expected to see. No wonder he'd been so bothered by what I'd said down in the living room. There was actually a part of him that thought his bank account was his only asset as a person.

"Don't be ridiculous," was what I finally managed to say. Not ideal, but it would have to do.

Suddenly, I was acutely aware of the electricity crackling in the space between us. We were sitting on a bed. It would be easy - *so* easy - to just lean over to him press my lips against his, and I was almost sure he wouldn't resist me. I could have what I wanted, if I could only find the courage to take it.

But what if he did resist?

What if he pushed back, saying *no, no, Maddy, I don't think this is a good idea.* Because it wasn't. But a part of me would always believe it was because I wasn't good enough for him. My ego was a fragile thing. I couldn't risk it.

But what if he didn't?

I could press him down into the fluffy, ridiculously luxurious bedclothes, and that's when he would resist, but not because he didn't want me. No, he liked to be in charge. About that, I was certain. He'd flip me over and hold me down by my wrists, growling in my ear, but when he loomed over me I'd see the wicked smile on his face. He'd kiss me until he forgot he was trying to restrain my arms and he'd let go then, his hands wandering all over my body, sliding under the light fabric of my blouse and pushing it up past my breasts. I'd lift my arms for him then, obediently, feeling the urgent twitch of him against my thigh. He'd pull the blouse over my head and toss it aside. I would bite my lip. My nipples would be so stiff he'd be able to tell how much I wanted him, even through the fabric of my bra. His lips would travel down my neck, his hot breaths sending little shivers down my expanse of bare skin...

I came back to reality with a start. I was staring at him, my mouth hanging open slightly. Luckily he didn't seem to be paying attention. Oh, my God. I had to stop doing this. I was going to drive myself crazy. I swallowed with difficulty; my throat had gone completely dry, and my heartbeat seemed to have relocated itself to somewhere between my legs.

I felt fuzzy and lightheaded, just like last night, but without the wine. Clearly, I didn't need alcohol to go completely stupid for Daniel.

He spoke, finally, still not looking at me. "Did you want to go home?"

"Yes," I managed. I stood up quickly, walking hurriedly down the stairs and gathering up my dress and jewelry. Daniel came down a few minutes later.

"The car will be waiting for you at the curb, whenever you're ready," he said. "No rush."

"Thanks for breakfast," I said, unable to look him in the eye for more than a few seconds. "And for last night."

"Of course," he said. "I'll...I'll call you." He looked almost as distracted as I felt. I gave him a little half-wave and hurried towards the door.

"Maddy, wait a minute." He reached into his pocket and pulled out a shiny key, looking like it was fresh from the locksmith. "I had this made for you."

"Okay," I said, walking back to him with leaden feet and taking it.

"Trust me," he said. "It'll look odd if you don't have it. You'd better get used to carrying it now."

The ride home seemed to take ages. I answered the driver's questions perfunctorily; yes, the date was very nice, yes, the food was excellent. Yes, the Inn had a lovely atmosphere. Yes, Mr. Thorne's apartment was gorgeous.

Just being back at home was a relief in and of itself, but I didn't truly relax until after I'd stripped out of the unfamiliar clothes and spent a little quality time with my removable massaging shower head. It was one of the few luxuries I allowed myself in life, and once I was finally sated, leaning against the shower wall with cheeks flushed and my legs turned to jelly, I prayed it would act as a sort of exorcism for my inconvenient desires. I'd been afraid to give in, even in this small way, but after this morning it was clear there was no turning back.

Once I was dried off and wearing my own clothes again, I spread the dress out on my bed and smoothed the wrinkles. It would probably need to be dry-cleaned. I laid the necklace and earrings next to it, straightening each little strand until they looked ready for a photo shoot.

They were beautiful things, to be sure, but they still didn't feel like mine. I wasn't sure I could ever truly immerse myself in a lifestyle where buying things like this was commonplace. It was so incredibly strange to me. The idea of money being some constantly renewable resource; technically finite, but the idea of spending all of it was incomprehensible. You'd have to buy a fleet of space shuttles, or an actual planet, to even begin spending it all.

I had to smile a little to myself at the idea of Daniel going to NASA and picking out shuttles as casually as if he were in a grocery store.

It was strange, though. For someone who'd been rich for as long as he had, he didn't seem to wear it too comfortably. It was rather curious, wasn't it?

But I couldn't worry about that now. Now, I had to focus on how on earth I was going to survive living with the 24/7 temptation that would be life with Daniel.

Chapter Six

It became normal for me and Daniel to eat

lunch together at work. It reached the point where he no longer had to call me; I'd habitually get up and walk to his office every day at eleven-thirty, and a subtly scowling Alice would take our orders. He must have eaten at every place in a ten-mile radius. He always had recommendations, and they were always good. Before long, he would greet me with a kiss on the cheek, right in front of Alice. I could practically feel her trying to strangle me with her mind. Oddly enough, all I felt was triumph.

"You know," I said to him one day, over a plate of falafel and shawarma, "all the women in the office absolutely hate me now." He looked up. "And some of the men."

He just laughed. "Well, that's not very charitable of them."

"I can't wait for the reactions once we get...engaged." I still had a hard time spitting the word out. "I'm going to need a police escort just to get to the copy machine."

"Eye daggers aren't actually deadly, you know." He tore off a piece of pita bread and dipped it into a little pool of hummus. "No matter how sharp."

"I guess."

"Are you going to tell your parents?"

There it was. I'd kept pushing that question to the back of my mind, but I was going to have to confront it eventually. "I'm not sure," I admitted, pushing some lettuce around on my plate. "We haven't really talked in a while. If I just call them out of the blue, and tell them I'm engaged..."

"They'll find out eventually, won't they? One way or another. Isn't it best that they hear it from you directly?"

He was right. The contract did stipulate that I had to change my relationship status on any social networking sites - which was only reasonable - and I was online "friends" with quite a few people who knew my parents. There was no chance I'd be able to skate by on that one.

Truth was, I'd kept most of my relationships secret from my parents. They were so probing and critical of most things I did, and I never wanted to go through all the hassle of trying to introduce them to someone, only to turn around later and inform them that we'd broken up. "But why? What happened? What did you do? Did you say something that scared him off? Maybe if you lost a few pounds...I mean, you're an attractive girl, but competition is fierce out there..."

I shuddered a little. The idea of telling them I was going to marry a billionaire only to tell them in a year that we were getting divorced...it was horrifying. But I had no choice, if I wanted to through with this. Surely two million dollars was worth enduring a few awkward phone calls.

We ate the rest of our lunch in silence that day. Daniel was aware he'd touched on a nerve, and he didn't bring the subject up again.

Late Friday afternoon, he came by my cubicle just as I was packing up my things. Thankfully, Florence had already cut out for the day.

"I'd like to take you to dinner tonight," he said, and there was something very meaningful in his eyes. Oh, God. This was it, wasn't it? He was going to propose to me. In public, I was sure. He had to make a spectacle of it.

"Okay," I said, my heart already fluttering in my chest.

"Be ready at seven o'clock."

The midnight blue dress was still in its plastic bag from the cleaner's, hanging in the back of my closet. I hadn't expected to need it again so soon. I pulled it out when I got home, quickly showered and dried my hair, and zipped myself up in it. It still looked fantastic, even when paired with a haunted, thousand-yard stare.

I wasn't ready for this. But I didn't exactly have a choice.

I clasped the necklace on and slipped in the earrings, pondering what I should do with my hair. Simply leaving it down didn't seem to befit the occasion, but it was stubborn. If I tried to put it up in something, I'd be fighting with it all night. The downside to naturally thick, glossy hair was that it was improbably heavy and slippery. I'd yet to meet a band or clip that could hold it, and I hated hairspray with a fiery passion.

Nothing for it, then. I brushed it thoroughly and let it fall around my shoulders, hoping I wouldn't look horribly out of place in whatever insanely expensive restaurant he was taking me to.

The driver was punctual as always, and this time, I was surprised to see Daniel already in the back seat waiting for me.

"Hello, Maddy," he said, looking at me approvingly. It had to be put on. No real date of his would wear the same dress more than once. But he hadn't said a word about it, so I tried not to worry.

"I'm sorry," I muttered, as I settled into the seat next to him. "This is the only fancy thing I have."

"Don't worry," he said. "You still look as stunning as ever."

I rolled my eyes.

The driver was watching us and chuckling to himself.

"She can't take a complement gracefully, this one," said Daniel. "It's tragic."

"Well, you'll just have to work on that, sir."

"I will, John. Don't you worry."

I sank deeper into the Italian leather and tried not to look miserable.

"What's the matter, darling?" Daniel said, finally, squeezing my shoulder gently.

"I don't know," I said. "I guess I'm just tired."

"Well, you'll forget all about it when we get where we're going."

There was something different in the tone of his voice, now that he was talking to me in front of John. Something a little...distant, maybe. Aloof? Uncaring, even. I was beginning to put the pieces together - how he must live large portions of his life, or maybe all of his life, striving to fulfill the expectations that were placed on him.

Poor little rich boy. I smirked at myself. Was I really trying to feel sorry for him? The man who could buy a space shuttle?

Man, I was really getting fixated on those shuttles. Maybe it was the summer moon shining so brightly every night that had me dwelling on space travel.

"Did you ever want to go to the moon when you were a kid?" I blurted out, sitting up straighter and looking at him.

His face broke into a smile - a genuine one. "What?"

"It's a simple question. Did you ever want to go to the moon?"

He shrugged. "It's just a rock. A giant rock out in the middle of nothing. What's to see?"

"Yeah, you know that now. But when you were a kid. Didn't you ever look at it, and marvel at how close it was, and think *man, I'd really like to go there*. It looks like it's so close, like you could just jump in the car and drive there in a few minutes." I looked out of the window; it was waxing, big and round, glowing just above the tallest buildings. "Doesn't it?"

"Honestly..." he squinted at it. "Well. Maybe."

"See? I used to imagine climbing the tallest trees around my house to try and get there. I knew it wouldn't work, even when I was little, but I just wanted to go there so badly. Just to do it. I don't know why. I know there's nothing there. I'd just like to be able to experience it, once in my life."

"Well, you know, space tourism is under development as we speak. You may yet have a chance."

Hell - he was right. If I was wise with my profits from this whole venture, I might be able to actually afford a trip to the moon someday. What an insane idea. My childhood dream, that I thought for sure would never come true. I really *could* have anything I wanted.

"I'll make sure to put it on my Christmas list," I said, leaning back in my seat.

The drive was a short one, taking us to a place downtown that I'd walked past many times, never even considering the possibility that I might eat there someday. It was sleek and elegant, more along the lines of what I had been expecting on our first date. While the Inn was lovely and comfortable, this looked more like the sort of place a high-powered businessman would propose to his supermodel wife.

Or me, as the case might be.

When we pulled up to the curb, Daniel jumped out of the car and quickly ran to my side, opening my door before I had a chance. He gave me his hand to help me out. As we walked arm-in-arm up the steps that led to the entrance, I could feel eyes on me.

I really should have gotten my hair done.

The host looked up and smiled when we walked in the door. "Mr. Thorne, we have your table right over here. Please follow me."

I had never felt more awkward in my life - and that was saying something. Walking between the booths and tables of the fanciest restaurant in the city, I tried to keep my eyes focused on the wall directly in front of me, but I knew people were watching me. Of course they were. Who wouldn't? I looked like a little girl playing dress up in Mommy's fancy clothes. It was absurd to think I could ever fit in an environment like this. No matter how much money Daniel spent on me, I'd always stand out as someone who was just pretending.

"Here you are, sir. Ma'am." The host handed us our menus. "Your server will be with you in a moment."

"Thank you, Tom." Daniel laid his menu down on the table, unopened. "Before you decide on anything, I recommend waiting to hear the specials. They're always seasonal and fresh as it gets."

"Thanks," I said. I didn't feel like looking at my menu anyway. I didn't feel like eating, for that matter.

The server came back shortly, prattling on about braised this and locally grown that. I ordered something I hardly understood, and he came back shortly with a bottle of white wine. As he poured us both a glass, I forced a smile at Daniel, acutely aware that we were being watched. Hopefully, if I looked strange, it would pass as the anxiety of a woman who was expecting to be proposed to, but was still unsure if it would really happen or not.

"Nice place, isn't it?" Daniel said, and I realized that I hadn't spoken in a long time.

"Yes," I said. "It's very...it's very classy."

"Not the sort of place you eat every day." Daniel poured himself a second glass of wine. "But, it's nice for special occasions."

"You *could* eat here every day," I said. "If you

wanted to."

He looked down at his napkin, unfolding and spreading it over his lap with exaggerated slowness so he wouldn't have to meet my eyes. To anyone listening it would probably sound like an innocent comment, but he and I both knew it was calculated to annoy him.

He didn't speak again until our entrées came. I had some sort of fish that was perfectly done, sweet and flaky, with crisp young asparagus and risotto on the side. I ate as much of it as I could manage, even though it seemed to turn to sand in my mouth. My throat was very dry. I finished the last of the wine, and Daniel gestured for another bottle.

After our plates were cleared away and we ordered dessert, he finally seemed to have relaxed a bit. He started talking again as if we were really just a couple on a date.

"Do you really want to go to the moon?" His eyes were sparkling with amusement.

"I mean...yeah. I thought everybody did."

He shook his head. "I don't think so. But I really hope you can, someday."

"I always wanted to go to space camp when I was a kid, but it was always too expensive." I laid my fork down on my plate, leaving my tiramisu half-uneaten. It was inevitable that there would be an awkward silence every time the topic of money came up. I wasn't sure which one of us was more to blame for it, but it was almost palpable every time. I shook my head and tried to think of an appropriate change of subject.

"Wasn't there something ridiculous you wanted to do as a kid?"

He pondered this for a moment. "Become a doctor?"

"That's not ridiculous."

"Well, neither is going to the moon, if you're cut out to become an astronaut. But for me, it was."

"Why?" I took a drink of my water. "I mean, seriously. What stopped you?"

"I got older, I suppose. I readjusted my expectations for myself."

The server came by with refills, and Daniel ordered a bottle of champagne. It was coming. I swallowed a rising lump in my throat.

"I don't see why you couldn't have done it," I said. "If you put your mind to it. You're obviously smart, so why not?"

He laughed, folding up his napkin carefully and returning it to the table. "Trust me, it's better this way."

I clenched my fists in my lap. I knew what was coming. I knew it, I'd known since the moment I signed the contract, yet I still wasn't ready. Far from it. I felt like I was going to laugh hysterically, throw up, and cry, all at once.

Daniel stood up.

His hand was in his jacket pocket.

I squeezed my eyes shut. When I opened them again, he was down on one knee.

He opened the black velvet box, displaying a delicate gold ring with twin diamonds nested together diagonally, complementing the wave design of the band as it ran underneath them. It was striking and subtle at the same time - stunningly beautiful, yet very wearable. I wondered if Emma had helped him pick it out. It seemed like her style.

"Madeline, will you marry me?"

I nodded, numbly. I had to close my eyes again. Tears were gathering, and I didn't know if I could hold them. My back ached as I sat bolt upright in my chair, keeping my eyelids glued shut, willing the tears not to come and ruin my makeup. I felt him take my hand and slide the ring onto my finger. It was perfectly sized. Of course. Daniel took my hands and pulled me to my feet, and then he kissed me. His lips were soft and warm against mine.

There was a smattering of applause. Daniel let me go, and I sat back down mechanically. The server poured champagne. I drank my whole flute in one swallow and tried to dab at my face with the napkin enough to dry it, without smearing my mascara.

Daniel was sitting down again, too. He

leaned across the table and spoke to me in a low voice. "Did you want to go home?"

I forced a smile. My eyes, at least, had stopped watering. Mostly. "No," I said. "I'm fine. It's just...it's a lot, you know?"

He nodded like he knew what I was talking about, but I wasn't sure that he did. From his point of view, it was just a fake relationship, a fake marriage. He was willing to go through absolutely anything to get what he needed. But for me, it was different. I couldn't explain why I was crying, to him or to myself. The maelstrom of emotions inside of me was impossible to understand in any rational way. I just knew that I wanted to cry.

I looked down at the ring, sparkling on my finger. It really was perfect. It was exactly what I would have wanted my real fiancé to pick out, if I hadn't given up on that idea a long time ago. Wait - was *that* what was bothering me? Really? I'd come to peace with the idea of being single a long time ago. This was the worst possible time to realize that I really did want to find my happily-ever-after, someday.

I took a deep breath.

It's just one year. It's just one year. It's just one year.

After that, I could do whatever I wanted.

"I think we'd better go home," said Daniel finally, apparently understanding that my *no* really meant *yes*.

We finished our champagne. My head was buzzing, and I was grateful for Daniel's arm to lean on as we made our way out to the curb.

John stared at me in the rear-view as we climbed in. "You feeling all right, ma'am?" he said. God, I must look like a complete mess.

"I'm fine," I sniffed. "Thank you."

"You ought to be congratulating us, John." Daniel took my left hand in his and raised it up, putting the ring on display for him.

"Oh my goodness!" John's face broke into a grin. "Congratulations, you two. That's so...it's such good news. I'm very happy for you."

"Thanks," said Daniel, draping his arm over my shoulders. John had come so very close to saying something about how quickly we were moving - I could tell - but it was his job to do nothing but nod and smile and validate all of his employer's choices. Just like everyone else in Daniel's life.

I knew Daniel was expecting me to spend the night at his apartment, and as much as I was dreading it, nothing else really made sense. We were a young couple, crazy in love, who'd just gotten engaged. We'd be expected to spend the rest of the night naked in each other's arms. We had to maintain the illusion.

When we arrived, I shed my shoes in the front entryway and walked straight into the main floor bathroom for a shower, not speaking to Daniel or even looking at him. When I got out, he was nowhere to be seen. I retired to the room I'd picked before, pulled two ibuprofens out of my purse and swallowed them dry, and climbed into bed.

I didn't cry. I felt completely empty and wrung-out, exhausted but unable to let myself drift off to sleep. I hadn't expected this to be so hard, so soon. Daniel was right. It was impossible to pretend we weren't human.

For the first time since I'd signed that contract, I truly regretted what I'd done. I felt caged. But even if I had the opportunity to back out now, would I? The carrot of two million dollars dangling in front of me was going to inspire me to keep moving forward, no matter how painful it was.

Well, the good news was it couldn't possibly get any worse than tonight.

Could it?

Chapter Seven

The next morning, after I groggily dragged myself out of bed, Daniel made me breakfast again. This time, he didn't need to ask me how I took my eggs. I ate mechanically and responded to him with one-syllable answers when he asked me how I was feeling, did I sleep well, did I have a good time last night? I could tell he wanted to ask much more prying questions, but he kept his mouth shut.

For a while.

Just as I was about to finish my second cup of coffee, he said:

"That was quite a performance you put on last night."

His eyes were searching my face. He knew it wasn't an act - he wanted me to admit it. He wanted to comfort me, just as if we were really a couple. Didn't he understand that was going to make it worse? We couldn't play at being in love in private. It was bad enough doing it in public, with everyone watching. At least then I could distract myself with the dubious thrill of deceiving people.

"Thank you," I said flatly, slamming my cup down on the counter so hard I was sure it would crack. It didn't, but Daniel jumped a little.

"I'm going to get dressed. Can you have John ready for me? I have to go home and take care of some things."

"Absolutely. Of course." I could feel him watching me as I walked down the hallway and disappeared into my room.

This was probably a bad time for me to sequester myself in my apartment and not speak to him or see him - it would look strange. But I had to appreciate that he wasn't pushing me. Maybe he did understand. Sort of. A little bit.

My apartment felt cold and strange when I got there. Oddly un-lived-in. I certainly hadn't ever gone on any sort of vacation or getaway since I'd moved in here, so it was an odd atmosphere. Until Daniel came along, I hadn't even spent the night at someone's place. I'd never felt comfortable doing it - it wasn't the intimacy of it so much as simply trying to sleep in a bed with another person. Of course the guys I usually picked had maybe a twin-sized bed if I was lucky, and getting a decent night's rest while tangled up with a sweaty, snoring, thrashing human being in close quarters was simply impossible. I didn't know how long-term couples did it. I needed my own space, a big, cool expanse of bed upon which I was free to sprawl as I pleased. I never felt lonely when I slept. Far from it.

Daytime was different, of course. Sometimes it was too quiet, a little too still, even for me. But that was the trade-off for independence.

It was going to be a rough adjustment to being a kept woman for a year.

Daniel didn't call me all weekend. My phone did ring once, but it was the mechanic, letting me know that my car was done and they'd send a courtesy shuttle to pick me up whenever I was ready.

It was funny; I didn't know they were open on Sundays.

The place was oddly deserted when the shuttle driver pulled in, and even when I craned my neck around the parking lot, my car was nowhere in sight.

The owner of the place came out to meet me.

"Here you are, Miss," he said, handing me an unfamiliar key.

I stared at it.

"This isn't mine," I said, even as the realization of what was happening grew in the back of my mind.

"With Mr. Thorne's compliments," the owner muttered, pointing to a car parked nearby. He looked as uncomfortable as I felt.

It *was* my car, technically, if my car were about ten years newer, and sleek black with silver trim.

"Same make and model, just a little bit of an upgrade," said the owner. "Mr. Thorne insisted. Said it was an engagement present."

I closed my eyes for a moment.

This wasn't happening. This could not be happening.

"He traded your car in for it," the owner went on, clearly trying to break the awkward silence. "Knocked a thousand bucks off the asking price."

"Thank you," I said, more loudly than I meant to. The owner stepped back, and I hit the automatic unlock button on the key fob. That was new.

Okay, to be fair, the whole car was new.

I slid into the leather seat and stuck the key into the ignition. It was such a familiar action, and yet so strange at the same time. It stank of new car. I rolled the windows down after I pulled out of the parking lot.

So it wasn't the most extravagant of gifts. To him, it was almost no money at all. But it was more car than I'd ever be able to afford. I'd bought the last one out of the classifieds for a pile of wrinkled cash. I hadn't ever tried to get financing for something at a dealership, but I had a feeling it would be a disheartening experience.

Somehow he'd known that buying me some hundred-thousand-dollar sports car would completely blow my mind, perhaps scare me off forever. He'd gone for a more subtle gesture. He was saying, *you can still have your old life, just...upgraded.*

Did he think that was what I was worried about?

As I pulled into my usual parking space at my apartment complex, I was acutely conscious of being watched. If one of my nosy neighbors said something about my new car, I was absolutely sure I'd have a complete breakdown right there in the hall. What was I supposed to say? "Oh, yeah, it's a gift from my fiancé." All cool and casual, like everybody gets brand new cars as an engagement present?

Once I was safe inside my apartment, collapsed in a chair, the guilt began to set in. I'd been given a really nice gift - maybe "generous" wasn't the right word considering the source - but it wasn't fair to Daniel to react like this. He hadn't done anything wrong. It was my own stupid fault I was getting carried away.

I took a deep breath and picked up my phone.

It rang once before he picked up.

"Hi, Maddy." He sounded tired.

"Thank you for the car." Oh, God. That sounded so ridiculous.

"You don't have to thank me," he said, and he sounded like he might be smiling a little bit. "But you're welcome. When I called them to check up on it, they gave me a further laundry list of problems that made it easier and cheaper to just buy something new. I didn't want to trouble you, so I just took care of it."

"Okay," I said. "But could you...not surprise me next time? It was a little weird."

"I'm sorry," he said. "Do you not like surprises?"

"Well, normally I don't mind." I fiddled with my ring. "But usually they're more like - 'oh, hey, I brought you this coffee from across the street because I happened to be there anyway.' Not like, 'oh, hey, here's a new car.'"

He sighed. "Maddy, I didn't mean to make you uncomfortable. I really am sorry. I just wanted to do something nice. I know this isn't an easy transition for you."

"It's okay," I said. "It's...it's a nice car."

"I'm glad you like it." There was a rustling noise, like he was switching his phone to the other side. "I did want to talk to you about something, if you have a minute."

"Sure."

"Next weekend, a few of my family are going to be coming into town. I let them know about you. I would have told you sooner, but I didn't think my sister and her husband were going to be able to get off work so soon."

"Oh," I said. I wasn't quite sure how I felt about that.

"They'll want to meet you, of course," he said. "But we don't have to overdo it. I'll tell them that you're very busy trying to get your affairs in order and plan for the wedding."

"It's all right," I said. And strangely, it was. The idea of meeting his sister's family wasn't nearly as terrifying to me as it ought to have been. Maybe I'd just maxed out on the amount of stress I was able to process, but I felt very calm. "I'd love to get to know them."

There was a moment of silence. "That's good," he said, sounding a little suspicious. "Well, I'll try to limit it to a lunch and maybe a shopping trip or two. I don't know exactly how long they'll stay."

"Don't worry about it," I said. "Really. I'm serious. It's not a big deal."

"All right, well." He exhaled. "I'll see you tomorrow for lunch, then."

"Okay. Bye."

"I love you," he said.

Did he really think someone might be tapping his phone? I shook my head.

"I love you too," I said, and hung up quickly.

Well, this was an interesting development. Meeting someone's family was always the best way to get to know the things about themselves that they weren't always forthcoming about. I was actually looking forward to talking to his sister. Maybe I'd actually learn something about the man I was going to marry.

I arrived at work the next morning in strangely good spirits. You might even say I was...glowing. Thankfully, that fit right in with my story.

"Oh my GOD!" Florence jumped up out of her chair and enveloped me in a fierce hug as soon as I walked into our cubicle.

"Congratulations! I can't believe it!"

"Yeah, me neither!" I squealed back, extricating myself from her grip with some difficulty. "We were keeping things quiet for a while, obviously, but..."

"So you won't be working here for much longer, probably. Right?"

I'd actually forgotten about that part. "Yeah, I mean...we haven't talked about it in a while, but I'll probably try to wrap up all my projects in the next few weeks so I can focus on planning the big day." Ugh. *Big day*? Had I really just said that?

"I'm so happy for you!" Annie settled back down in her chair, thank God. "Is somebody throwing you a bachelorette party? Because my cousin is part-owner of that male strip club down on the ave, I could probably hook her up with a discount group rate."

"Oh, I don't..." What was my excuse going to be? I don't have any friends? That sounded hideous - plus, she might actually offer to throw it for me. That was obviously unacceptable. "...I don't really go in for that kind of thing." I fidgeted a little, trying to look as much like a prude as I possibly could. I wasn't, really, but the idea of a bunch of meatheads gyrating their sweaty pelvises in my face while I sucked down fifteen dollar drinks wasn't exactly appealing.

Annie looked at me, her eyes narrowed. I

needed a better excuse.

I leaned forward, lowering my voice a little. "I just...I don't really think Daniel would be too happy about it."

Understanding dawned on her face. "Ohhh," she said. "Okay. I get it. Little bit of a jealous type, huh?"

I shrugged, smiling a little. "I dunno if I'd say *that*."

"Hey, there's nothing wrong with that! Personally, I think jealousy can be pretty hot."

Ugh.

Thankfully, the chatter stopped once she fell into that interminable vortex that was her inbox. Florence's habit of signing up for everything and never remembering to check the "do not email me" box was the inspiration for most of her workday complaints, but for once, her chronically overstuffed email was working in my favor.

I managed to make it until lunchtime with only three more attack-hugs and awkward conversations, and I was able to avoid eye contact on my way to meet Daniel for lunch.

We ordered Chinese food - from the only four-star Chinese restaurant in town, of course. To be fair, it *was* pretty damn good. And at least it still came in those nice familiar cartons.

"How's your day going?" Daniel wanted to know.

"Well, Florence tried to offer me a discount on male strippers, so...pretty decent?" I broke an egg roll in half.

"Fantastic," said Daniel. I thought I saw a brief shadow pass over his face in response to something I'd said - but no - I must have imagined it. "No one's talked to me yet. I'm not sure why."

"Abject fear?" I twirled some noodles onto my fork. "Well, I sincerely hope someone offers you a discount on female strippers before the day is out. I wouldn't want you to miss out on that experience."

He chewed silently for a moment. "I did talk to my sister earlier. She wants to take us all out to dinner with her husband when they get in."

"Great," I said, with a smile that wasn't even a little bit forced. "I can't wait to meet her."

"Really?" He was giving me a look.

"Really," I said, lightly. "I think it'll be fun."

I wasn't sure why he was unnerved by the idea, but for some reason, that just made me more excited to meet her.

-

I'd hovered over the "relationship status" bar for way, way too long. It was time to make the change.

Then again, I hadn't told my parents yet.

Then again, was I going to?

I'd been going around in circles like this for

ages. I had to make a decision already. As much as I wanted to simply change my status and move on, I knew I needed to tell them first.

It took me five tries to dial the number all the way.

Once it started ringing, I almost lost my nerve and hung up, but instead, I waited.

"Hello?"

"Hi, dad," I said.

"Oh," he said, sounding vaguely stunned. "Maddy. Hi. How are you?"

"I'm...I'm good." I took a deep breath. "Is mom around?"

"Yeah, want me to get her?"

"Could you both get on the phone? I want to tell you something."

"All right." He sounded suspicious, but he did what I asked nonetheless. I heard my mom's voice in another few moments.

"Hi, honey," she said. "How has everything been?"

"Pretty good," I said. "I just got engaged."

Silence reigned for a few seconds. Then, they both started talking at once.

"Who are you-"

"You didn't tell us-"

"It happened really fast," I said, quickly. "It's my boss. His name is Daniel."

"At that...office supply place?"

"No, mom. That was years ago. I'm at a

consumer electronics place now."

They digested this for a moment.

"Well, at least he'll be able to support you, then," was my dad's contribution.

"Yes," my mom pitched in. "I always hoped you'd find someone who would be able to provide for you so that you could pursue your...art."

I squeezed my eyes shut. "Thanks, mom. Listen, I have to go. I have a lot to do. But I'll send you guys an invitation to the wedding, if you want to come. It's not going to be a big deal, nothing too fancy, but Daniel can take care of your travel costs." I knew there wasn't a chance of them coming if they had to pay for it themselves.

"Oh..." said my dad, clearly searching for the right words. "No, honey, I don't think I'll be able to get away from work. And your mother's not supposed to travel, you know, with her hip."

"Yeah," I said. "I just thought maybe...well, I'll send you some pictures."

"That'll be very nice," said my mom.

After I'd hung up, I was left with the distinct feeling I shouldn't have bothered.

The next week went by in a blur. I was trying to tie up as many loose ends as I could, finishing projects, or at least getting them to the point where my replacement wouldn't want to kill me. The H.R. department was taking interviews. I was trying not to think about leaving. As frustrating as my job could be sometimes, it was still going to be strange, not coming in here every day.

On Friday, my desk phone started ringing. Which was...odd. I picked it up.

"Hello?"

"Maddy, hi." Daniel cleared his throat. "Could you, uh, step into my office, please?"

I could have sworn I heard someone talking in the background. I frowned slightly. "Is something wrong?"

"No, no, nothing's wrong, just...can you come over here?"

"All right, fine."

When I reached his office, the door was closed. This time I was sure I could hear voices in there.

"Go on in," said Alice, from her desk in the hall. "They're waiting for you."

They?

I pushed the door open and walked inside.

Daniel was sitting behind his desk as usual, but there was a couple sitting in the chairs opposite him. They were surrounded by baggage on the floor around them. The woman had no sooner looked up than she jumped to her feet and ran over to me.

"Maddy!" she exclaimed, throwing her arms

around me. I hugged her back, realizing this must be Daniel's sister, but why on earth hadn't he at least given me some advance notice before calling me in here to be ambushed?

She was laughing.

"I'm Lindsey," she said. "Daniel's sister. This is my husband, Ray."

Ray waved, smiling politely. He looked like he wasn't too terribly thrilled about the ambush, either.

"I'm sorry," Lindsey said, not looking all that apologetic. "Our flight got in early and we couldn't check into our hotel yet, so I decided we should come surprise Daniel. I wouldn't let him warn you."

"That love of surprising people runs in the family, huh?" I grinned at Daniel, who actually looked...*embarrassed*? Oh, this was going to be fun.

"What's this?" Lindsey's eyes darted between us, a conspiratorial smile on her face.

"Well, the other day...I thought I was going to pick up my car from the mechanic's, and he'd bought me a completely new one," I said.

Lindsey burst out laughing. "Seriously? Danny never was one for surprising people when we were growing up, I'm glad to hear he's starting to see the fun."

Danny?

This just kept getting better and better.

"We still need to settle in, obviously." Lindsey's eyes drifted to the bags on the floor. "But I hope you're both free for dinner tonight. We're taking you out to the nicest place in town."

Daniel cleared his throat. "We were just there not too long ago," he said. "I think we could use a little variety."

Lindsey waved her hand in a dismissive gesture. "The second nicest place, then. Or the dive with the greasiest burgers, I couldn't care less. I just want to get to know my new sister-in-law."

"Greasy burgers sounds great, to be honest," I said. "I'd love to eat someplace where I can wear jeans."

"Perfect!" Lindsey went over and clasped Daniel on the shoulder, jostling him gently. He flinched a little, and then smiled. "What do you think, Danny? Jerry's Grill? I bet it's just like the one back home."

Daniel chuckled a little. "Really? We haven't been to one of those in…God. How long's it been?"

"I'd rather not think about it," said Lindsey. "I just remember you always used to throw a fit whenever Dad wouldn't let you get a milkshake."

She looked at me then, for some reason, and I wasn't sure what I was meant to say. "Too much sugar?" I supplied, trying to imagine Daniel as a little kid bouncing off the walls because somebody let him have too much candy.

Lindsey frowned a little. An awkward silence reigned for a few moments.

"Burgers sound great," Ray piped up from his chair. "Six o'clock?"

Daniel opened his mouth to object, but Lindsey shook her head, instantly silencing him. "Shut up, Dan. Nobody else likes to wait until the crack of midnight to have their dinner. You can just take it to-go if you absolutely have to wait until the most fashionable hour to eat."

I giggled. I couldn't help it - I'd always hated that he wanted to take me out to dinner so late, but I figured that was just how it was going to be with him. He commanded so much quiet authority. But not, apparently, when his sister was around.

A familiar melody, tinny but clear, echoed through the room.

"Oh," said Lindsey, reaching into her pocket. "That'll be the hotel. We'd better go meet our shuttle."

"I'll help you with your bags." Daniel got to his feet, but Lindsey stopped him with a single look.

"For Christ's sake, Danny. My arms work." She chuckled. "See you at Jerry's at six!"

Once they were safely down the hall, I turned to look at Daniel. He had the thousand-yard stare of a bomb survivor.

"She's quite a firecracker," I said.

"I'm sorry," he said, quietly, not looking at me.

"No, I like it." I pulled one of the chairs over and sat close to his desk. "I like her. She doesn't take any bullshit, does she?"

He finally cracked a smile. "No," he said. "No she does not. Least of all from me."

"I can't wait for tonight," I said. "Seriously."

Daniel looked relieved. "Lindsey's cultivated a certain personality," he said. "To get by. To thrive, really. She runs the biggest architectural firm in Boston. You don't get to where she is by playing nice with men like me. It's a reflex by now, I think." He shook his head. "Anyway, she's my big sister. She's allowed certain liberties."

"I should say so."

It made perfect sense, now - someone with Daniel's ambition but without the advantage of his XY chromosome would naturally develop Lindsey's personality. I could tell from the tone of his voice that he admired his sister, perhaps with just a touch of that awe that younger siblings tend to carry for their older brothers and sisters, even when they should, by all rights, be equals.

"It really will be fun to have dinner somewhere casual," I said. "Don't you think?"

"I suppose." Daniel was shuffling papers on his desk. "How's it going out there? Do you almost have everything wrapped up?"

"I guess," I said. "You know, you'll never find another designer quite like me." I was mostly kidding, but I suppose a part of me was fishing for a compliment.

He smiled wryly. "Get back to work, Ms. Wainright. I'll come by for you at five thirty."

"I'm going to need to cut out early if you want me to have time to get home and get ready, *sir*," I said, with exaggerated politeness.

"Of course. Go home at four and relax."

"Oh, *thank* you, sir."

He shook his head. "You're picking up a bit of my sister's bad attitude," he said. "I'm not sure I like it." But he was smiling.

"I'm so sorry, Mr. Thorne. I'll make sure to work on it."

And with that, I sashayed out of his office.

Chapter Eight

We arrived at Jerry's Grill right on time, and Lindsey and Ray were waiting for us on the bench outside. Lindsey waved enthusiastically with both hands, pulling me in for another half-hug like she hadn't seen me in weeks. "You'll love this place," she said. I loved the smell already - one hundred percent authentic beef and fry oil.

It was noisy and hectic inside, but our smiling hostess led us on a long, winding pathway to an empty booth near the back of the restaurant. Unlike many of the faux-Americana burger joints that had sprung up modeling themselves after places like this, the black and white photographs and memorabilia on the walls were all authentic. I'd heard of this place before - it always garnered a mention on those food-centric travel shows, and had a top spot on "iconic places to eat" lists for my city. People were always surprised when I said I'd never been, but there wasn't much money to eat out when I was a kid. And as an adult, going to place like this alone just seemed...sad. It was the kind of place you'd bring your family.

After we sat down and ordered a round of sugary alcoholic drinks - I almost wanted to burst out laughing when Daniel agreed to a pitcher of strawberry margaritas - I actually began to feel relaxed and at home for the first time since Daniel had "proposed" to me. Lindsey soon launched into the epic saga of her most absurdly difficult client, and we were all laughing uproariously even before the margaritas started flowing.

"...and then he goes, 'well, *you're* supposed to be the expert!'"

Lindsey was wiping tears from the corners of her eyes, and I was right there with her. Back before I'd landed this job, I used to do a lot of work on the side for absolutely impossible people, because I simply couldn't afford to say no. It was comforting to know that even people on Lindsey's level still struggled with such things.

Of course, I'd never have to do anything like that again, if I played my cards right.

"Well, you won't have to worry about that for much longer," Lindsey said after a moment, like she was reading my thoughts. "Lucky, lucky."

"Yeah," I said, staring into my drink.

"Well, I wouldn't ever want to quit work anyway," said Lindsey lightly, pushing her drink aside as the server came back with our orders. "I'd go crazy. I'm like one of those sheepdogs that always needs something to occupy my time, or I'll destroy everything. Oooh, who got the bleu cheese burger? That looks fantastic."

We dug into our food, and the conversation fell silent for a while. I kept glancing at Daniel. It was strange to see him in a place like this, and stranger still to see him not looking uncomfortable in the least. Even with barbecue sauce dribbling down his chin, he was somehow still the man I knew - and yet, utterly *not*.

I was deathly curious to know more about his childhood memories of this restaurant. They were obviously bittersweet, perhaps more bitter than anything - but that didn't kill my curiosity in the slightest. I had a feeling if I could get Lindsey alone, I might be able to learn a little bit.

"Mmm," said Lindsey, setting her burger down in its basket to wipe her hands and face. "The burgers here haven't changed a bit. I love it."

"That's because they've never cleaned the grill," Daniel said, dryly.

Ray looked down at the burger in his hands. "Gross," he said.

"All the best burger places don't," I supplied. I was pretty sure I remembered seeing something about it on a T.V. show about the world's greatest diners. "It gets so hot that nothing ever goes bad, so all the flavor stays on there for years and years."

"You'd better be kidding," said Ray, downing the rest of his margarita.

"Deadly serious," said Daniel. "She's right. It's nothing to worry about, don't you think the health inspectors would have said something about it by now if it was?"

Ray shook his head, regarding the burger

hesitantly for a moment, but then he shrugged and raised it to his mouth again.

"And the burger wins out!" Lindsey grinned. "The burger always wins out, doesn't it?"

"If it's the right burger? Absolutely." I broke a huge steak fry in half and dipped it in ketchup.

"Maddy." Lindsey leaned across the table. "I know you're busy, wrapping up work and planning the wedding and everything, but can I take you shopping tomorrow? Just us girls. Those two can hang out and toss a football around in a parking lot or whatever the hell they do. I've been doing a little independent research, so I know all the best vendors and boutiques. I'd love to take you around. What do you say?"

I grinned at her. "I'd love to!"

By the time we all left Jerry's, everyone was in a happy mood. Daniel and Ray were joking around with each other, and Lindsey was telling me about all the ridiculous mishaps from her own wedding ceremony and planning process. I hadn't actually given any real thought to the whole thing - I supposed Daniel would go along with whatever I wanted, but I didn't know *what* I wanted.

"...the point is, no matter what happens, everything will be fine. We can talk more about it tomorrow. I know it's stressful as hell, the industry puts all this pressure on us, but there's no reason why it has to be a big old mess. Especially not with me helping you out."

She hugged me goodnight, and then we all parted ways. I found myself getting into the town car with Daniel and not even questioning where we were going; I'd spend the night at his place, of course, and that was all right with me.

The next morning, Lindsey came by at ten o'clock on the dot. We started out with breakfast in a trendy vegetarian diner - "I'm not vegetarian, obviously, but sometimes I like to pretend" - and then hit the fancy shopping district.

"So do you have a dress picked out yet?" Lindsey wanted to know. "I got the impression that Daniel wanted to have the wedding sooner rather than later. He hates anticipation and long-term planning. Always has."

I shook my head. "I figured I'd just pick something off the rack. Doesn't have to be a 'bridal gown,' you know? Just something nice."

"Yeah, that's for the best. Some of these places, they tack another eight hundred dollars on the price tag of anything that's 'for a wedding.' I know it doesn't really matter, but I object to it on principle."

I nodded. "I really just want to keep things casual." This was true; I just couldn't reveal why. "I want to marry Daniel because I love him, not because I want to have a Big Day. You know?"

Hell, I was almost convincing myself. Well done.

Lindsey was nodding. "I can see how you two ended up together," she said. "He's never been that much of a romantic - or a traditionalist, I guess. You know what I mean." She hesitated. "How do your parents feel about the whole thing?"

The inevitable question. I paused for a moment. "They're not really...I haven't exactly told them yet."

"Oh," she said, understanding dawning on her face. "I'm sorry, I didn't meant to bring up something difficult. We don't have to talk about it."

"Thanks." As much as I was growing to like Lindsey, I didn't really feel like discussing my awkward situation with my parents with anyone, least of all someone I'd just met.

We visited a few bakeries, more than one stationery shop, and a few dress places, just to try things on. Looking at myself in the endless mirrors, I felt next to nothing. It was just me in a big fluffy white dress. I wasn't a bride. I was just playing a part.

"I'm surprised I can fit into my normal size, after those burgers last night," I commented as we left one of the dress shops.

"Tell me about it." Lindsey laughed. "Worth

it, though, right?"

"Always." I hesitated. "So, you guys used to go there a lot when you were kids, huh?"

"Not as much as we would have liked to." She turned to look at me. "Has Daniel told you very much about his childhood?"

I shook my head. "Almost nothing."

"I figured as much," she said. "He doesn't like to talk about it. That's his way of coping, I guess." She was silent for a moment. "I don't mean to make it sound like our family life was some kind of horror show. It wasn't really all that bad. But it was hard, sometimes. We didn't exactly have a lot of money to spread around in the early days. The first time Dad took us out to Jerry's Grill, it was because we came home from school early - there was a problem with the gas lines or something, I don't even remember now - and we walked in on him with another woman. He promised to take us out for burgers if we kept our mouths shut. Being a couple of little brats, of course we kept demanding to go back every time we were unhappy, or he did something we didn't like. I feel terrible about it now. I'm sure Dan does too. But we didn't know what we were doing at the time, really. Kids are selfish. We just wanted to eat something for dinner that wasn't out of a box from the discount store. I have no idea how my dad scraped the money together to keep taking us there, but he found a way."

I had no idea what to say in response to all that. My head was swimming. I just nodded silently and waited for her to continue.

"My mom never found out, as far as I know. I guess it was better that way. I don't know if my dad kept doing it. They were both young, and I realize now that I'm not sure if they ever really loved each other. It could have very well been a shotgun wedding. For years, I shied away from close relationships because of what they'd taught me through example. Thank God I met Ray. He stuck by me even when I tried to push him away." Her eyes were very far away as she spoke. Finally, she turned back to me. "I've got to say, I was really happy when Daniel told me that he'd found someone. I was afraid it would never happen for him. I think the whole situation affected him more than it did me. It's hard not to get cynical about love, coming from a background like that."

"Yeah," I said. "Believe me, I know. I mean…I don't know if my parents cheated on each other, but they definitely weren't in love."

Lindsey nodded. "There's a lot of that going around, isn't there? People getting married for every possible reason, except for the right ones."

Tell me about it.

I wanted so badly to tell her, then - to just

blurt out the truth. But I knew I wouldn't be able to handle the way her face would fall, realizing that Daniel hadn't found his true love after all. I had to let her believe we were happy together, at least for a little while.

I was horrified to realize tears were welling up in the corners of my eyes. I forced them back, swallowing the lump in my throat and walking forward.

"Anyway," said Lindsey. "Enough of this depressing crap. Have you picked a venue yet?"

"No," I admitted. "To be honest, I've been putting a lot of things off…it's just so overwhelming, but I know it's not going to get any easier the longer I wait."

"That's what I'm here for!" said Lindsey. "Why don't we head back to the apartment and start looking at places online. We're going to want to narrow it down before we start driving all over the state looking for the perfect place."

We headed back to Daniel's, and I was suddenly grateful for the key he'd left me with. The doorman smiled and nodded in recognition as we walked past. Once we were inside, Lindsey made a bee-line for the fridge and poured herself a glass of juice. She was infinitely more at home in the place than I felt.

"Now, where does Dan keep his laptop?" she wanted to know.

Oh, *shit*.

"Um...it's hard to say, he kind of takes it all over the place with him," I fibbed. God, I had no idea.

"Well, we'll just have to search then. Why don't you check the bedroom? I'll look down here."

I was halfway up the stairs before I remembered the very obviously lived-in guest room down there.

Shit, shit, *shit*.

I had to keep going. I couldn't act suspicious, or like we were hiding anything. If she said something, I'd just explain that I wasn't...used to sleeping in a bed with someone else? Maybe? Oh God, would I be able to say it with a straight face? My face was already burning.

I searched through the bedroom blindly. There could have been ten laptops in there and I might not have noticed. I came back down the stairs slowly, empty-handed of course, and saw Lindsey standing the middle of the hallway, looking confused. Hopefully just because she couldn't find anything.

Or...not.

"Hey," she said. "So did you guys - have someone over recently?"

I tried to pretend like I was confused for a moment. "Oh! You mean, in the guest room? That's my stuff." My own voice sounded like a strange, distant echo in my head. My heart was pounding. "I'm just not used to sleeping in the same bed with somebody, you know?"

There was a beat of silence.

"Oh, of course," said Lindsey. "I was the same way with Ray at first. I'd never spend the night with him when we first got together, it drove him crazy."

"I'm glad you know what I'm talking about," I said, feeling my anxiety level ratchet down a few notches. "Some people would think it's weird."

She waved her hand dismissively. "Don't worry about it. Whatever you've got to do. Did you have any luck up there?"

"No," I said. "But, I'll go look again. I actually forgot to check in the closet. He keeps his laptop bag in there, maybe it's still packed up."

I had no idea if any of this was true, but I needed an excuse to go back and actually check the bedroom now that my brain was functioning again.

And a good thing, too - it was sitting on the dresser, in plain sight. Lindsey would have thought I was the biggest flake in the world.

"Found it," I called out, coming down the stairs.

"Oh, fantastic. Let's see what we can find."

Pretty soon, we'd pulled up every wedding vendor list, registry, and search result in the entire city. My head was swimming, but Lindsey seemed to be digesting the information just fine, taking copious notes in a little pad that she'd produced from somewhere. Another family trait, it seemed.

"All right," she said, after what felt like hours. "So I've eliminated every place that we definitely don't want, which leaves us with about twenty choices. Personally, I'm a big fan of the art gallery. Have you ever been there?"

I shook my head.

"Oh, my God, we *have* to go," she said. "They're closed today, but soon. It's absolutely gorgeous. Of course you have to hire their overpriced caterers, but they'll take care of absolutely everything. And there's no cake-cutting fee." She rolled her eyes.

"Cake-cutting fee?" I stared at her. "Is that...is that a thing?"

"Trust me," she said. "They'll nickel and dime you for everything in this industry. You've got to keep your wits about you."

There was so much I didn't know, and simply didn't have the desire or motivation to figure out. I didn't know what I would have done without Lindsey. Hire a wedding planner, I supposed. I'd almost forgotten for a moment that it was easy enough to solve these sorts of problems just by tossing more money at them.

"Lindsey," I said, straightening up on the

sofa, "can I ask you something about what we were discussing earlier?"

"Sure," she said. "What do you want to know?"

"You said, growing up...there wasn't a lot of money. So what changed?"

She chuckled a little. "You won't believe me when I tell you. Dad hit it big at the casino. I mean, really big. I still think he was trying his damnedest to gamble away everything he had...mom had just passed, and in spite of everything I guess he just didn't know what to do without her. But instead of losing, he won the biggest jackpot they'd ever had. His picture's still on the wall, if you go there - a sad sack in flannel and overalls, just holding up this novelty sized check like it's a death sentence. After that, he turned everything around. He could have squandered it all, but instead he went downtown and handed a pile of cash to a financial planner. I never knew him to be like that - but I guess something about having all that money just scared him." She let out a long breath. "A few good investments later, we found ourselves moving into a nicer house in a much better neighborhood, and suddenly we weren't hoping and praying for scholarships and applying for tiny scraps of federal aid anymore. We could go to any college we wanted. After all these years, I still think back on that time and how strange it was. It was like a waking dream. You know?"

I did know. I knew all too well.

"Wow," I said.

"Wow is right." She stood up. "I'm guessing you're more than a little bit familiar with the feeling, though."

"Yeah," I said. "Going from all my credit cards maxed out and bills overdue, to this..."

Speaking of which, my credit cards were still maxed out, and quite a few of my bills remained overdue. I'd been so busy focusing on adjusting to my new life that I had completely forgotten to ask Daniel about the possibility of taking care of a few of my immediate financial needs. I should probably get on that.

"I know," she said, resting a hand on my shoulder. "It'll feel strange at first, but eventually you'll adjust to it. And you don't have to become one of those obnoxious Old Money-type people who wear skirt suits to the country club and yell at their cleaning ladies. Just keep your head on straight, you'll be fine."

I smiled at the mental image. "Thanks," I said. "But can I at least get a little dog to carry around with me?"

"Whatever you like, hon." She grinned. "The world' s your oyster now."

Chapter Nine

Ray had to get back to work, so all four of us visited the art gallery on Monday morning, and then we bid them goodbye. Lindsey had been right - it was gorgeous, with a massive hall of historical sculptures and statues that they recommended for the ceremony. They were surprised when Daniel said he wanted to book it "as soon as possible," but they were able to get us a date in a month. He put down a deposit, but he wouldn't let me look at the full quote.

Lindsey left me with pages and pages of notes. Daniel had already put Emma on the task of finding me a dress, and I'd picked a bakery whose cake was both beautiful *and* edible. Even with all of the preparations that were underway, the whole thing still didn't quite feel like real life. But I was sure I would adjust to it. Eventually.

I put in my last day of work on Friday, and Daniel asked me over lunch if I wanted him to hire a moving service. As usual, he was ten steps ahead. In the flurry of wedding preparations, I forgot that I'd also be expected to move in with him immediately afterwards.

"No, I'm fine," I said. "I don't really like strangers touching my stuff."

"At least let me come over and help you pack." He sounded genuinely concerned.

"All right, sure. Thanks." He wasn't a stranger, after all. He was my fiancé. A thought occurred to me. "Hey, are we like...going to go on a honeymoon, or something?"

The corner of his mouth quirked up into a secretive smile. "Just leave that to me," he said.

-

Between shoving all of my worldly belongings into boxes and returning vendors' phone calls, the next few weeks went by in a blur. I finally heard back from Emma, sounding almost breathlessly excited, telling me she had the perfect dress. She refused to text me a photo, insisting that I see it in person first. So I came by as quickly as I could, in the car that still didn't feel quite like mine, feeling intensely awkward as I parked it in front of the boutique. It was hardly nice enough to be conspicuous, but it was so far from anything I'd ever driven that I couldn't get used to it.

Emma looked like she was about to go nuclear from happiness.

"Come on, come on!" She put her arm around my shoulders and herded me into the dressing rooms as soon as I stepped through the door. "I've got it hiding back here, I didn't want anyone else asking about it. And God forbid Daniel should drop in and see it."

"I'm not superstitious," I said.

"Oh, honey." She shook her head at me. "Everyone is superstitious when it comes to weddings. You might as well get on board."

I rolled my eyes, but she was too elated to notice. "Look at it!"

The dress was hanging up in front of me. It was sleek and elegant, without all the taffeta and usual trappings of a typical wedding dress. Yet, at the same time, I felt I would be recognizable as a bride when I put it on. It was a lovely cream color, with deep red accents, including a sash around the waist.

"I figured something short would be best for a summer wedding," Emma said. "So? Do you like it?"

"It's beautiful," I said, reaching out to feel the material. "I just...none of this feels real to me yet, you know?"

"I know," she said. "Come on. I can't wait to see it on you."

She helped me into it, having me step into a pair of complementing shoes after she zipped me up. I stared at myself.

This was what I'd be married in.

Emma gasped. She looked more emotional about this than I felt.

"It's really nice," I said, lamely. "Thanks, Emma. I couldn't have done it without you."

"Doesn't even need a single alteration," she

murmured, walking around in me in circles and touching and tugging at various parts of the dress. "Even *I* didn't think it would be this perfect."

"And you're so humble, too." I smoothed the dress over my hips one more time, as if it would somehow cement the idea that this was really happening.

"Shut up. You love it." She turned towards the door. "Don't move, I'm going to find you some accessories."

She came back with some lovely silver pieces that matched the red accents - *were those real rubies?* - and before long I was out the door, and on my way to the hairdresser's to settle on a style for the "big day." I hated that phrase, but with everyone around me using it at least three times per hour, it was inevitable that it would become a regular part of my vocabulary.

I hadn't had a hot iron in my hair since prom, and I almost wanted to choke on the smell of all the hairspray. But at the end of it, with all my hair piled on my head and my tiara on top, I actually looked like a bride.

As time went on, it was even starting to feel real.

The weekend before the wedding, Daniel came over to help me pack, as he'd insisted. Mostly everything was in boxes already, and I was going to send over everything I didn't absolutely need for the next few days. Together we spent the better part of the morning loading up a U-Haul, and every time he hefted a box I felt bad for not just letting him hire a moving service. But he didn't even show a hint of complaint or frustration with the process, even when I did.

I ordered pizza for lunch. I was becoming a lot less self-conscious about my choice of eating establishments, which was nice. He seemed to enjoy it as much as I did, and while we sat holding our slices on my empty living room floor, I figured it was as good a time as any to bring up my faltering finances. It was more awkward than I had expected - then again, with me, everything usually was.

I talked circles around it for ages, until he finally prodded me to just spit out what was on my mind.

"I have a few bills..." I started, and he raised his hand to tell me I'd said enough.

"Just give everything to me," he said. "I'll see that it's taken care of."

"Some of them aren't...small," I said. "And when I called to cancel my utilities, they threatened collections if I didn't take care of everything within 30 days."

"Don't worry," he said. "It's going to be all right."

And suddenly, I knew that it was.

Until that moment I hadn't realized how much I'd worried about this - even though it was ridiculous to do so, I'd fretted over how he might respond, how he'd feel about the fact that I was being so needy and demanding before we were even technically married. Not to mention how many sleepless nights I'd spent before he came along, wondering how the hell I'd ever manage to pay everything off by myself. I could actually feel the muscles in my shoulders relax slightly, after being held tense for God knows how long.

"Thank you," I said, perhaps a little too fervently, judging by the surprised look on his face.

"Maddy," he said. "This was part of our arrangement. I'd take care of you financially during this time. It's the least I can do, you don't have to thank me."

"It's just...I've been so worried for so long, wondering how I was going to ever get out of debt. And now it's gone. I don't have to worry anymore."

"That's right," he said, smiling. "No more worrying."

I still have no idea why I thought it was a good idea to lean over and kiss him. Perhaps it was meant to be a friendly peck, or maybe in the back of my mind I thought someone might be peering in through the window.

Or maybe, just maybe, I couldn't help myself.

For a moment, he was still; surprised, I supposed, at my forwardness. But the hesitation only lasted for a split second before I felt his hand slide around the back of my head, pulling me in aggressively, and it seemed the only appropriate response was to let my lips part against his.

He took the invitation immediately, his tongue slipping into my mouth and exploring the territory, and I felt a shiver of pure bliss run down my spine. Within moments, I was completely lost in him - forgetting where I was, and why I was here. I was throbbing. I needed him more than I had ever needed anything.

I leaned into him, deepening the kiss even further. When we broke apart to catch our breath, I expected him to say something - to object, even if it was just half-hearted - but his eyes were dark and fierce and single-minded. There was nothing in his face but pure lust.

I melted. He coaxed me down onto the carpet with the movement of his body, stretching over mine, until he was lying on top of me. I could feel him rock-hard and straining in his jeans. Oh, God. This was really going to happen.

My head was buzzing with arousal and disbelief, and to this day I still don't know what possessed me to look him directly in the eye and say, in a breathy voice:

"Thank you."

The look on his face made my heart sink.

He pulled away, his expression twisted with something like disgust. At me? At himself? I didn't know. I wasn't sure I wanted to. I sat up quickly.

"What's wrong?" I felt frantic. I was so close to having what I wanted, and he'd ripped it away from me. Why? What had I done?

He shook his head, looking at the floor. "This isn't a good idea," he said, flatly.

Well, no shit it wasn't. I sat up quickly. "You didn't seem to care a few minutes ago," I said, starting to feel desperate.

"I lost my head for a second," he said. "I'm sorry. I really am. But we can't do this."

I sat, miserable and motionless, on the floor as he gathered his things. He'd been planning to drive the first load over to his apartment after lunch anyway, but something told me he wouldn't be back again today.

After he shut the door behind him, my massaging shower head got the workout of a lifetime.

Once my head was clearer, I became determined that I wasn't going to let that happen again. If he was going to have an attack of conscience just because I said something silly, well, that was his problem. Did he really think I was the kind of person to have sex with someone purely out of gratitude? Had he not been able to tell how aroused I was? How badly I wanted him? He was an idiot to walk away from all that, no matter how complicated it might make our arrangement.

The next morning, bright and early, my phone started to ring. I let him call a few times before I picked up.

"I was going to come over in half an hour with the truck," he said, without so much as a greeting. "If that's convenient for you."

"Sure," I said, coolly.

The pizza box was still on the floor when I walked out into the living room. I crushed it angrily and shoved it into the garbage.

When I opened the door, he actually looked a little bit sheepish.

"About last night," he started, and I cut him off with a raised hand.

"Don't worry about it," I said. "I was out of line. No explanation necessary."

He seemed to accept this, but as we packed up the rest of my worldly belongings, I could feel him watching me carefully.

After he dropped me back off in my mostly-empty apartment, I walked through the suddenly unfamiliar rooms in silence for a while before collapsing on my bed. It was one of the few things that didn't need to come with me - of course.

But if he thought I was actually going to sleep in his bed with him after yesterday, he was crazy. I wasn't sure if that had ever been in the cards. I'd thought about it, of course - several times, and in exquisite detail - but unless I wanted it to end like yesterday had, it was obviously best if we never let ourselves get that close.

When I answered the door, he didn't even look up. He walked in silently, picked up a box, and walked back out again.

Okay. So that's how it was going to be.

On the last trip, I followed him out to the U-Haul and climbed into the passenger seat. He glanced at me briefly, but didn't say a word. I figured I might as well start unpacking and settling in.

It was a bit of a shock to see his apartment with my boxes scattered all over it. It was no longer exactly a candidate for an interior decorating magazine. He'd left most of the stuff on the main floor, but I noticed some of the boxes were up in the loft area.

Might as well rip that Band-Aid off right now.

"Why is my stuff up there?" I pointed.

He looked at me like I'd sprouted a second head.

"You don't expect me to sleep in your bedroom, do you?" I clarified.

He blinked. "You *did* read the contract, didn't you?"

Had that really been in there? Oh, man. I really should have hired a lawyer.

"You've seen the bed," he said, dryly, beginning his trek up the staircase. "It's a king size. We'll hardly even have to see each other."

I briefly considering picking up the vase of bamboo from the entry table and throwing it at his head.

I started digging into the boxes on the main floor. I'd expected my stuff to look dowdy and out of place, but now that I was actually faced with the prospect of unpacking it, I had a crazy urge to throw it all in the garbage and start over. What had I been thinking with some of this shit? Mugs full of pens? A ceramic dog from my trip to England when I was eleven? At the very least, I should put it all into storage. It had no business being here.

I rifled through all the boxes, looking in vain for something that I wouldn't be embarrassed to bring out. Paperclips? Three boxes of paperclips? Why did I even have these? And two brand new six-packs of sticky notes. What the hell did I think I was, a one-person office supply store?

When Daniel came back downstairs, I was

sitting cross-legged on the middle of the floor, surrounded by crumpled-up newspaper. I had ink stains all over my hands, and I was examining an unopened package of multi-colored permanent markers.

He sat down next to me, and, miracle of miracles, actually spoke.

"You've got yourself a nice collection of office supplies there," he said.

I nodded.

He didn't speak for a little while longer, but I was acutely aware of the soft, even sound of his breathing. He was so close, just inches away.

"I'm sorry," he said. "About what happened yesterday."

"Me too," I lied.

He picked up a pen and uncapped it, examining the tip like it was the most interesting thing he'd ever seen.

"I didn't mean for things to get out of hand," he said. "It's not a very good start for us, is it?"

"Our relationship hasn't even really started yet," I said. "Officially."

"I know. I'm sorry I left. I just figured it was best if I..." he squeezed his eyes shut for a moment. "Maybe it's better not to talk about it," he said, finally. "Just know that I'm sorry, and I won't let it happen again."

"Sure," I said. "To change the subject, how do you feel about throwing all of my stuff in a giant bonfire?"

"Seems like a waste of effort," he replied, smiling. "Should've done it before we went to all the trouble of bringing it over here."

"Before *you* went to all the trouble, you mean."

"I was happy to help," he said. "I mean it."

"Okay."

He looked over all of the mess one more time. "You know, if you want an office space, we can convert one of the guest rooms."

"What would I do there?"

"I don't know. Whatever you want."

"Maybe not an office so much as a…studio," I said. "Some place where I can work on my art."

"Of course," said Daniel. "Anything you want."

I had to smile at him. I wasn't quite finished being irritated about the whole after-pizza incident, but he was being awfully nice. Of course, it was in his best interests to keep me happy. I had to remember that.

Don't let things get too personal.

Well, that was going absolutely stellar so far.

I sighed, re-packing all my office supplies. "So these can go into the spare bedroom, I guess. I don't know about the rest of this crap."

"Well, you don't have to decide right now," said Daniel, charitably. "When we get back from the honeymoon you'll have as much time as you need to unpack."

It must have bothered him, all of these ugly, disorganized boxes invading his impeccable space, but he didn't say a word about it. I had to give him credit for that. He wasn't trying to be difficult. It was just a difficult situation. And maybe I'd made it harder than it needed to be, by coming on to him so strongly the day before. Maybe I *did* feel just a tiny bit remorseful.

Still, though. There was no reason for him to be such a baby about it.

"Yeah, I think maybe I'd better focus on the clothes for now," I said. "I assume that's what's upstairs?"

"Mostly," he said. "Come on, let's take a look."

We spent the next few hours organizing my clothes. He even helped me decide what to get rid of and what to keep, promising me I could rush-order some new stuff online when we were done, so it would get here in time for the honeymoon. He didn't even raise an eyebrow at how many frayed and hole-ridden clothes I still had, stuff I'd bought before college, the sorts of things that no billionaire's wife should ever be seen wearing.

After that, I got to shopping. He sat me down on the sofa with his laptop, and handed me his credit card. It looked normal - for some reason, I'd been expecting something heavy and jet-black, like the legendary no-limit card that was said to be accessible only to the very wealthy and influential. But this was just fine. He was just a normal guy, after all.

"Have fun," he said, winking at me. "There's no credit limit."

Or...maybe not.

Chapter Ten

The morning of the wedding dawned warm and clear, a pink sunrise bleeding across the sky. I woke up too early and couldn't get back to sleep. Of course.

The only things I had left in my apartment were a few clothes and other necessities, most of which I'd already packed for the mystery honeymoon. I wished he'd just tell me where we were going. All of this secrecy made it almost seem...romantic. Like we were a real couple. Clearly, we didn't need any help getting ourselves confused on that front.

I'd spent the whole day before cleaning every inch of my apartment, in accordance with the three-page-long list of demands my landlord had sent over. Apparently, I wasn't going to get my three hundred dollar security deposit back if

I didn't give the place the white glove treatment. Of course I didn't care about the money anymore, but I needed something to do. Anything to take my mind off of the future.

So there was nothing to do on my wedding day except sit and think.

My stomach was in knots. I made myself a cup of mint tea and sat by the window, watching the empty sidewalks slowly fill up with people. I had an appointment at the hair salon in a few hours, and I was going to meet Lindsey there. She was going to stand beside Daniel as his "best man." I had no one. Not even my father, to walk me down the aisle.

But that was fine. I'd walk down the aisle by my own damn self. I had two million dollars waiting for me at the end of it.

I had to stop getting caught up in stupid, pointless sentimentality. This was a fake wedding, for God's sake. There was absolutely no reason to get emotional over it. Weddings were a con to begin with, clearly. The soaring divorce rate spoke to that. I was just helping Daniel take advantage of a very convenient loophole in the immigration laws of the United States that allowed for couples to stay together, if they were willing to sign a piece of paper. It was as simple as that. People did it all the time.

My resolve thus steeled, I drove to the salon with my head held high. If I seemed distant, people would simply write it off as nerves. I had nothing to worry about. I just had to get through the day, and after that, things would settle down into some version of normalcy that I hadn't quite figured out how to achieve yet. But I knew that I would.

Somehow.

Lindsey chattered at me the whole time we were getting our hair done. I nodded and smiled, but didn't hear a word of it. None of this meant anything. None of it mattered.

Walking through the marble archway of the art gallery, I was struck again by how breathtaking the place was. They had set up pew-style seating and laid out a long, red carpet for me to walk on.

I wandered aimlessly through the gallery until Lindsey chased me down, insisting that it was time for me to change into my dress. I'd completely lost track of the hour. I realized I hadn't seen Daniel all day, and I told her so.

"Don't worry," she said. "He's coming."

As if he wouldn't.

I was kept sequestered after that - God forbid anyone should see *THE DRESS* - but Lindsey wouldn't stop offering to get me things. Water? Champagne? Food? Juice? More food? I hated to keep saying no to her, but I really felt if I ate something I might throw up.

When I heard the music start playing, my

stomach actually lurched.

Lindsey rushed in.

"Okay, we've got about ten minutes until go-time. How're you feeling?"

"Sick," I said, truthfully, staring at my reflection in the mirror. I tried to arrange my face into something that looked a little more like happiness, like I was marrying the man I loved. I vaguely succeeded.

"I have to go take my place," Lindsey said, after a few moments. "Just take some deep breaths. The band will switch over when they see you coming."

I sat there alone, waiting until the clock ticked over to the next hour, and then stood and walked out into the hallway.

My shoes clicked on the marble floor as I approached the carpet, and everyone turned to look. I was clutching my bouquet like a shield. I forced myself to stare straight ahead, looking at the officiant standing behind the pulpit, focusing on just putting one foot in front of the other. I didn't dare look at Daniel.

I didn't dare.

But I did.

He met my eyes and smiled - a little hesitantly, but his intent was obviously to give me courage to go on. I had to appreciate that. Lindsey was beaming next to him. I wondered if his conscience was eating him alive, lying to her like this. Mine certainly would, if I had any family who actually cared about me.

I forced a smile as I reached the front of the hall. Daniel took both of my hands and held them gently as the officiant spoke. Thankfully, we weren't doing any complicated vows. I just had to say "I do" when I was prompted. I was pretty sure I could handle that.

"...in sickness and in health...as long as you both shall live?"

Shit, I hadn't been paying attention. Which one of us was he talking to?

I waited for a beat. Daniel watched me expectantly.

Me, then. Okay.

"I do," I blurted out.

"You may kiss the bride."

I barely felt it when his lips pressed against mine - briefly, but long enough for the whole place to erupt in cheers.

We held hands and ran, handfuls of flower petals raining down on us from the guests - that was a nice touch. Daniel pulled me aside, into the room where I'd gotten dressed, closing the door behind him.

I don't know why I was expecting him to grab me by the shoulders and shove me up against the wall, kissing me passionately and telling me how much he wanted me. I knew it wasn't going to happen. Instead, he pulled out a chair and sat down, resting his elbows on his knees and rubbing his temples.

"Well, we survived that much," I said, helpfully.

"Yes," he said, dully. "But there's still the reception."

"With food and drinks," I reminded him. "So...silver lining, huh?"

He let out a huff of laughter. "I don't think I could eat now if I tried."

"Yeah, me neither," I admitted. "So...what? Should we just leave and let them assume we wanted to start the honeymoon early?"

"They're already assuming that," he said. "Everyone saw me drag you in here. Let them. I just need a minute to clear my head."

"Just one minute?" I smiled. "You might want to wait a little longer than that, to keep up appearances."

He gave me a withering glance.

"Sorry, sorry," I muttered. "Trying to bring a little levity to the situation."

In the end, we did end up going to the reception. My stomach had settled a little, so I ate a few tiny sandwiches and downed a great deal of champagne. I talked and laughed with everyone I knew, and some people I didn't know. I recognized quite a few faces from the office (including Lisa, who I studiously avoided) but Daniel had somehow managed to fully populate the place, and as I worked my way around the room, I learned they were from every imaginable time and location - business connections, former accountants, even one of his business professors. Daniel certainly did a better job of keeping up with people than I did. Either that, or people were much more apt to drop everything and run to the wedding of a billionaire they knew than some girl they barely remembered.

As the night waned and the guests began to stifle yawns, I changed into a more casual dress - a sporty black number I'd ordered after Daniel gave me his card - and got my bags ready. John was waiting outside to drive us to the...airport, probably. Hell if I knew.

Daniel was in much better spirits as we climbed into the backseat of the town car, guests yelling their well-wishes after us. He even smiled when I put my hand on the back of his neck and pulled him into a kiss. For appearance's sake, of course.

After a short while on the highway, it became obvious that we were indeed going to the airport. Well, I'd know where we were headed soon enough. He couldn't keep it hidden forever. All he'd told me so far was to pack for warm weather, and that hardly narrowed it down very much.

Then, John bypassed the usual pick up/drop

off points, going around through a back road that said "AIRPORT STAFF ONLY." I started to speak, but Daniel shook his head.

"Don't worry," he said. "I've made special arrangements."

I settled back in my seat. Well, then.

The road was narrow and winding, until it finally opened up...right on the tarmac. There was a plane parked in front of us - small, but still commercial-sized.

So that was how he planned to keep the surprise going. A chartered plane. Of course.

The brilliant bastard.

"I don't suppose there's any chance that somebody's going to tell me where we're going," I said, as Daniel and I crossed the tarmac, with John carrying our bags a few feet behind us.

Daniel shook his head, smiling, as John handed the bags off to someone standing by the bottom of the staircase that led up to the plane's entrance.

"Have a good trip, you two," said John, waving.

The inside of the plane was lavish and roomy, with white leather seats and every imaginable amenity. After we'd settled in, a platinum blond attendant took our drink orders, and before long we were soaring in the clouds, headed for an unknown destination.

"Will you at least tell me how long the flight's going to be?"

"Long enough," he said. "You'll want to settle in."

He wasn't kidding. I'd only been on planes a handful of times in my life, but I'd always had trouble sleeping on them. This plane, though, was a different situation entirely. I could lean back as far as I wanted, curled up in the luxurious seat. Before I knew what was happening, Daniel was shaking me awake.

"We're about to land," he whispered, smiling.

When we disembarked, the heat was the first thing I noticed. It was thick and humid. There were palm trees in the distance.

"Welcome to Florida," the captain said, as we left.

Well, then.

"I hope you're taking me to Disney World," I told Daniel as we got into our taxi.

"No," he said. "Better. But first, we're going to the hotel to settle in."

A five-star hotel, naturally. I don't know why I would have expected anything different. We were in the honeymoon suite, on top of everything, so it was massive, and had its own Jacuzzi. I felt like I could get lost just inside our room. It had a dining table, for God's sake.

"What do they think we're going to do, entertain guests?" I wondered aloud, running my hand along the polished wood surface.

"Maybe we're supposed to 'christen' it," Daniel suggested with a half-smile. He'd come a long way - he was actually willing to joke about us having sex again.

I pulled my hand away quickly.

"Don't worry," he said. "This is a nice hotel. They actually clean *all* the surfaces."

"That's not what I read once in an email forward," I called after him as he disappeared into one of the other countless rooms.

I had a very welcome shower in the lavish bathroom, which had more water pressure than any other hotel I'd ever been to, combined. And it didn't even smell like feet. Was this how the other half lived?

When I'd freshened up, I went out to meet Daniel in the main living area. He was flipping through the channels on the massive flat-screen television.

"Anything good on?"

"Is there ever?" he said. "Come on. We've got an appointment with someone I think you'll want to meet."

So he was determined to stay mysterious, then. Fine.

We got into another taxi for a short drive. As we drew closer to what was apparently our destination, I saw a massive white building in the distance. It was almost as wide as it was tall.

I thought it looked vaguely familiar, but we were apparently approaching it from the back, so I couldn't see any identifying signs or markings.

Then, finally, something came into view.

A giant American flag.

And, on the other side, the NASA logo.

"You're not actually taking me to the moon, are you?" I said, staring.

"Sadly, that's not possible yet," he said. "Not even for me. But I got you the closest thing I could."

As the car pulled up to a door on the side of the building, I saw a woman walk out. She came towards the car with purpose.

After I climbed out, she offered me her hand.

"Hi," she said. "You must be Maddy. I'm Sam - I'm an astronaut."

"That's...that's cool," I said, dumbly.

She grinned. "A few years ago, I was the first woman to walk on the moon," she said. "I hear you're something of a moon enthusiast."

"I wouldn't say that," I replied, a little stunned. "But I guess...I guess I always did kind of want to go there. It just looks so cool."

"It's pretty cool," she said, grinning. "If I could really take you there, I would. But since I can't, I'm going to give you the next best thing. Over the next three days, I'm going to put you

148

two through a simulated astronaut training. Everything you'd do if you really were going to the moon. At the end, we'll do a simulated landing and moon walk. It's a new attraction - not open to the public yet, but when Daniel here wrote to us and told us about how he wanted to give you your dream vacation, we couldn't resist the opportunity. We wanted you to be the first to try it out."

I didn't know what to say.

"Are you pumped?" she asked, sounding pretty pumped herself.

"Yeah," I said. "I just...yeah. This isn't what I expected at all." I could feel myself grinning from ear to ear.

"That's a good thing, right?" said Sam. "The unexpected things are always the most fun."

"Oh, absolutely." I glanced at Daniel. He was beaming.

We walked inside then, slowly. I had to drink everything in. This had honestly been the last thing I'd ever expected - that he would remember what I said about wanting to go to the moon, and that he'd make an attempt to fulfill my impossible childhood dream. How much thought had he put into this? How much time had he spent? The money, I knew, was nothing to him. He could have given me any lavish gift in the world, any generic multi-million dollar vacation. But this was something else.

This was the sort of gift you give to someone that you truly care about.

The training, Sam informed me, wasn't to start until tomorrow. Today, we'd just take a tour of the astronaut hall of fame, taking in all the exhibits - the old space suits, the models, the photographs. Sam told us about her personal experiences as we went.

"When I heard they were doing another manned moon landing, I was one of the first to put my name in," she said. "A woman had never walked on the moon before. I couldn't resist the opportunity. Of course, every other female astronaut had the same idea. But of all the names, they picked mine." She took a deep breath, her eyes distant for a moment. "I'll never forget, as long as I live, how it felt to put my foot down on that rock. Some people told me I was crazy for even caring about it - just a pebble floating in space, nothing really special about it. I can't really explain why I wanted to go, but it was the most breathtaking experience. To see the earth like that. The stars. To be in space. It was my dream come true."

Briefly, I wondered if I was turning green.

"But enough about me!" Sam said, suddenly. "Come on. Let's show you the rest of the facility. There are some pretty amazing things that don't get shown on the regular tours, but

I'd be happy to take you there."

With every step, I felt more and more like I must be dreaming. What kind of fake husband would go to this kind of trouble? There was an answer of course, in the back of my mind, quiet but persistent; I had to shut it down. *No, no, no. He pushed you away. He doesn't want you to get attached. He doesn't have feelings for you; he just wants you to be happy so you don't try to get out of the deal.*

We passed through the touristy areas, and soon Sam was taking us through doors that said "AUTHORIZED PERSONNEL ONLY." I held my breath as we stopped to look at instrument panels and control rooms, while Sam rattled off things that only halfway made sense to me.

When the tour was over, Sam handed us each a schedule for the next few days, detailing what we'd be doing for the next few days for our "astronaut training." Reading over it in the back of the cab on the way back to the hotel, I felt giddy. So maybe this wasn't quite what I would have imagined - but it really was the best of all possible honeymoons.

Chapter Eleven

Somehow, in my absence, I'd almost forgotten how beautiful our suite was. I was struck again as we walked in and Daniel hit a switch, lighting up the chandelier in the center of the room.

"This is really nice," I said, stupidly.

He smiled. "I'm glad you think so."

I stood in the center of the room for a moment, hugging my arms across my chest. I needed to say something. I needed to tell him what was running through my head, even if it didn't make any sense.

I needed him.

I couldn't even look at the massive bed, covered in overstuffed pillows, without imagining him pressing me down into it.

"Daniel," I said.

He turned to look at me. I didn't know what I was planning on saying, exactly, but every word that came to mind just stuck in my throat. I swallowed and tried again, and to my absolute mortification I realized tears were leaking out of the corners of my eyes. I tried to look away, but he came over to me, swiftly, gently taking my face in his hands and lifting it up towards his. I tried to smile, but it wavered.

"What's wrong?" he asked softly. "I mean...you know. Apart from the obvious." He, too, was trying to smile and not quite succeeding.

"Nothing," I said, in a voice thick from crying. *Well, that was convincing.*

"Really," he said. "Why don't I believe you?"

I laughed a little, through my tears. "I'm sorry," I said. "I'm really sorry."

"Please don't apologize."

I shook my head. "Not for that. I'm sorry for...letting things get too personal." I sniffed. "You know what I mean."

"Please don't apologize for that, either," he said. "I shouldn't have...I never should have..." He hesitated. "I'm sorry," he finished, finally.

"Maybe neither one of us really has anything to be sorry for," I said.

"Maybe," he said, with a spark in his eye that made my fingertips tingle.

"It was stupid, right?" I said, blinking the last of the tears away. "Saying we wouldn't let things get personal? Of course it's going to get personal. It's only natural. There's no harm in that, is there?" I cleared my throat. "I mean, as long as we keep our heads on straight."

"Can we?" He looked...skeptical. And, at the very same time, he looked like he didn't really want to be.

I shrugged a little. "Does it matter?"

He looked at me, his lips parted just slightly. Like he wanted to say something, but he didn't know how.

"Are you sure?" he said, finally. "Are you...absolutely sure?"

I went up on tiptoes and pressed my lips against his.

At that moment, it was like something snapped inside of him. More so than when I'd kissed him before - now I realized he'd been holding himself back even then. I could feel it in his body pressed against mine, in his touch.

I realized he was moving, propelling me backwards, until I felt myself pushed against the wall while his mouth devoured mine. He let go of my face and grabbed my wrists, hard - almost to the point of hurting - raising my arms up against the wall too, pinning my hands above my head. I felt deliciously helpless. Something inside me, a heat that had been growing since the first time I'd laid eyes on him, grew and grew. My blood felt molten in my veins. If he didn't touch something other than my wrists soon, I was going to explode.

He pressed his knee between my thighs.

I moaned, feeling myself swell against the hard muscle of his leg. He finally let my wrists go. I grabbed him by the shoulders, pulling him impossibly closer.

Just when I thought he couldn't kiss me any deeper, he found a way. When he finally pulled back, we were both panting, and I thought back to the night in my empty apartment and I was suddenly very afraid.

But he only smiled and took my hand, pulling me into the bedroom.

He stopped at the foot of the bed to kiss me again. I couldn't remember the last time I'd just *kissed* someone for such a long time - or maybe it had just been a few minutes, I couldn't tell anymore. The ticking of the grandfather clock in the dining room seemed, by turns, to be going very very fast, and then very very slow.

When he finally stopped, again, my lips felt bruised. Every breath seemed to short, like I'd never catch it and completely fill my lungs again.

His mouth quirked up into a half-smile.

"Relax," he said. "Breathe."

Was it that obvious?

I tried, but it wasn't easy. My heart felt like it was trying to escape from my ribcage. Every part of my body was tingling, aching for his touch. All I felt was urgency and need.

"I can't," I whimpered, hating how pathetic I sounded.

"Yes, you can," he said, gently. "Focus on your desire. *Be* with it. And just breathe."

I closed my eyes. Finally, I felt myself begin to un-tense my muscles. I refocused on the throbbing feeling in my core instead of trying to shrink away from its intensity. When I opened my eyes again, I was finally able to take a long, deep breath.

"There you are," Daniel said, smiling, brushing his fingers against my flushed chest. "It's very important, in moments like this, to remember how to breathe."

Just the light touch of his fingertips on my skin was enough to make me part my lips and exhale with pleasure. I'd never felt anything like this before. When he reached down and raised my shirt up over my head, the mere slide of the fabric against my skin was enough to make me shudder.

I'd never imagined it could feel like this. I must have been a ball of tension and nerves every other time I'd had sex, because this was unprecedented. I'd never realized. As simple as it was, I'd never tried to just *breathe* before.

He seemed inordinately pleased with himself, judging by the expression on his face. I almost wanted to laugh, but at the same time, I didn't.

"It's deceptively simple, I know," he said. "You've never heard that before?"

"What? To just breathe?" I gasped as he rested his hand on my breast, pressing against the taut nipple. "No. I guess not."

He brushed my hair behind my ear. "Stick with me," he said. "I'll teach you all sorts of things."

"That's very magnanimous of you."

"Oh," he breathed, inches away from my

lips. "It'll be my pleasure."

He kissed me again, just a brush of his mouth, strangely chaste. Then, he reached behind my back and unfastened my bra. He pulled it off and tossed it aside.

His eyes raked over my body and I almost felt it like a physical touch. Finally, his fingers settled on the button of my shorts, and undid it.

They fell to the floor. I stepped out of them, feeling strangely without shame, standing there in the middle of an obscenely expensive hotel room in my panties.

"Don't forget to breathe," he said, teasingly, kneeling down slowly on the carpet. I had to concentrate, as his own hot breath tickled skin. It brushed across my lower stomach, my hipbones, and lower -

His fingers slid under the fabric of my panties and pulled them down, slowly.

His face was inches from my sex. I was losing focus. *Breathe. Just breathe.*

He leaned closer and pressed a hot, open-mouthed kiss on my hip.

I moaned a little. I knew exactly what I wanted him to do, but at the same time, I was afraid if he really did it, I'd scream, or collapse, or both. My knees already felt weak. When his tongue flicked out and traced the crease between my thigh and my mound, mere inches from where I most wanted it, I shivered and heard myself begging.

"Please," I whispered.

He looked up at me and smiled.

"All you had to do was ask."

At the first lap of his tongue, I pitched forward, grabbing his shoulder for support. He held on to my hips and pulled back. "Shhh, shhh," he said. "I've got you. Just breathe."

I kept leaning on him, taking long, shuddering breaths like he'd told me to. When I was able to let go of his shoulder and stand on my own again, he leaned in and continued his ministrations.

This time I was able to keep my balance, although every muscle in my body twitched and shivered at the exquisite feeling of him. Because I was focusing so closely on not falling over, the sensations somehow hit me more slowly, crawling through my nerves instead of slamming into me, the way pleasure normally did. I was filled with a delicious ache. I let my head fall back, my eyes closing as I let out a long, shaky moan.

My fingers rested against the top of his head, scratching lightly at his scalp. He hummed against my swollen flesh. Rather than an ever-rising, unstoppable build towards climax, I was feeling something different. Deeper. The feelings ebbed and flowed, but even the ebbs made my toes curl into the carpet with pure bliss.

He picked up his pace, slightly, which I hadn't even realized I wanted; but as soon as he did, I moaned again, rocking forward. But this time I kept my balance. I managed to keep my feet flat on the floor, taking in the pleasure instead of letting it overcome me. I felt like I was glowing from the inside.

When I came, it was something that rose up from deep inside of me, stronger than anything I'd ever felt before. But I never lost myself in it. I stood strong in it, like a sailor tied to the mast of a ship, letting the feelings wash over me until I couldn't hold them all inside any longer.

Then, I screamed.

When he stood up, wiping his face with one hand, I was still upright, somehow. Still standing. My legs ached, but at the same time, I couldn't remember ever feeling this good.

With a sudden movement, he picked me up, bridal-style, and carried me over to the bed, dropping me on the mattress with a devilish grin. I fell, laughing, in a heap.

"Now," he said, looming over me on the mattress, like I'd dreamed of so many times. "Wasn't that a good time?"

I nodded, biting my lip. "Want me to return the favor?"

His eyebrow quirked. "What do you think?"

I laughed, reaching down to cup the straining

hardness under his jeans. "Yes? No? Maybe?"

He rolled off of me and stretched out on his back, giving me full access. As much as I wanted to undress him slowly, to drink in every inch of him, I also felt compelled to focus on the part of him that seemed to need my attention most urgently. I unzipped his jeans and yanked them out of the way, dragging his underwear down with them. My breath caught a little in my throat.

But at the same time, my mouth was watering.

I leaned down and licked the whole length of him, finally taking everything I could fit into my mouth and caressing him with my tongue. He sighed and arched his back, his eyes half-closing. I wondered if he'd imagined this. Of course he had. How many times, I wondered? Was it his favorite fantasy? In his imagination, how did he like me best?

I bobbed my head up and down, trying to keep my eyes on his, watching every little twitch of every muscle in his face. I didn't want to miss a moment of this.

He warned me before it was over - very gentlemanly - but I didn't mind taking it all in. He was my husband, after all.

We lay silently together for a while after that, with nothing but the sound of each other's heartbeats. I didn't know what to say. I wasn't sure if it was wise to say anything at all. I certainly didn't plan to get back from the honeymoon and pretend this never happened, but I had a sneaking suspicion he might expect me to. Or worse - he'd want to be friends with benefits throughout the duration of our marriage, only to end everything after the divorce?

Wait - was that a bad thing?

Wasn't that exactly what I'd expected, when I let myself give in to this? Okay, so maybe I'd wished we could ever be a real couple. I was finally willing to admit that to myself. But I'd known it was never going to happen. I'd gone into this understanding that the best possible outcome involved the very thing I was now afraid of.

I could have Daniel for one year, or I could have him for less. Those were the only possible options.

The knowledge of this weighed heavily on my mind while we ate our room service dinner, quietly, in front of the T.V. I wondered if Daniel was thinking similar thoughts - trying to figure out how he was going to cut me loose without causing too much of a fuss.

No, that wasn't fair. It wasn't fair, but it was all I could think.

I lay awake for a long time that night. Even though I was far enough on my own side of the bed that I barely knew he was there; but at the same time, I was acutely aware that he was really inches away from me. I finally fell asleep after what felt like hours of staring into the unfamiliar darkness of the room.

I felt groggy and discontented the next morning, but I hoped that my first day of "astronaut training" would at least be enough to keep my mind off of all the things I didn't want to think about.

When we first arrived, Sam welcomed us with a breakfast of genuine astronaut rations - surprisingly edible - and an overview of everything we'd be doing for the day. It started with lighter activities like a mission briefing, fitting into jumpsuits, and our "career assignments." Apparently, "astronaut" wasn't quite the specific term I'd always assumed it to be. Within it, there was a wide range of different skills and specialties. Mathematicians, scientists, engineer - all of them pilots, but from such different walks of life I wondered if any of them had started out wanting to be graphic designers. Maybe my wires had gotten crossed somewhere. Maybe I should have been one of them.

Then I would have actually made enough money on my own to make this whole thing unnecessary. Then I could have actually done this for real, instead of just pretending.

By the end of the day, I was tired and overwhelmed. I collapsed in the middle of the massive bed when we returned to the hotel, closing my eyes against the lights. A few minutes later, I felt the mattress dip as Daniel sat down beside me.

"I was thinking we might go out for dinner," he said. "If you're feeling up to it."

"Sure," I said, because I had no reason not to. But really, all I wanted was to curl up in bed and be alone for the rest of the night.

We ended up going out for sushi, at a five-star place of course. I was actually starting to feel comfortable in places like this. I'd grown to realize that no one was actually staring at me, like I'd assumed. As long as I held my head high and acted like I belonged, everything would be just fine.

Daniel used chopsticks like an old pro. I don't know why that surprised me. When we got back to the hotel, I was feeling in a considerably better mood - whether because of the good sushi or the good sake, I didn't really care. We laughed and joked on the way back to the hotel, tumbling into bed just like a real honeymooning couple. We kissed and undressed each other slowly, and that night I saw him naked for the first time. I let my eyes wander all over him, memorizing every inch of his skin. I didn't know what was going to happen when we got back, but I realized it was foolish not to enjoy this while it lasted.

I couldn't remember the last time I'd just relaxed in bed with a lover like this; not in any particular hurry, just letting the moments drag themselves out. I remembered to breathe. Long, slow breaths.

"Where did you learn that thing?" I asked him, letting my nails drag lightly up and down his chest. "About breathing?"

He smiled. "If you ask me, too many men have a fixed mindset about sex. They believe they're pretty much born instinctively knowing everything they need to know, and if they have to seek any kind of outside knowledge, that's somehow a form of failure. I never bought into that. I fumbled through things when I was a teenager like everyone else, but once I grew up, I wanted to really learn how to do it right. So I did what I'd do for anything else - I took lessons from an expert."

"A sexpert." I had to admit, it was a smart thing to do - but the idea still made me giggle.

"Laugh all you want," he said. "But she taught me how to get the most out of every experience. For me and my partners."

"I'm not laughing at you," I lied. "I just…it's pretty cool. Most guys won't do that, like you said. Unless somebody drags them there."

"It's silly," he said, as I ran my hand up and

down his thigh. "The odd hang-ups people have about trying to improve themselves, sexually. I mean, why not? We take lessons for everything else. Nobody expects that you'll be a prodigy at anything else without some training."

I got up on my knees and straddled him, carefully, reaching for the condom sitting on the bedside table. "Do you usually tell your partners about your...training?"

"My work speaks for itself," he said, his breath hitching a little when I grabbed his rapidly hardening manhood by the base and squeezed a little.

"And so humble, too," I said, rolling the condom down over his velvety-soft skin.

"To answer your question..." he paused as I sank down onto him, my inner heat enveloping him eagerly. "....no. I don't think...." He exhaled. "....they'd necessarily understand."

I nodded in agreement before throwing my head back and losing myself in the rhythm of riding him. He couldn't tell any woman he actually cared about, because they might shrink at the idea of a man purposefully taking sex lessons. But with me, it didn't matter. With me, there was no risk.

With me? Nothing to lose.

I banished these thoughts from my head, focusing all my efforts on grinding my hips, watching for the particular movements that made his jaw clench and his eyelids flutter. When I purposefully tightened my inner muscles around him, he groaned softly. I'd forgotten how much fun this was, having a man completely at my mercy.

Suddenly, his expression changed. He was refocused. Watching me carefully. His eyes narrowed.

"You're enjoying this a little too much, aren't you?"

Chapter Twelve

I gaped at him.

"You're enjoying this a little too much, aren't you?"

What on earth was that supposed to mean?

"You're enjoying it too," I said. "…aren't you?" He obviously was, but I had no idea what he was driving at.

"Being on top," he said. "Literally and figuratively."

I stopped moving. "All right," I said. "Did you…did you want to switch positions? Or what?"

Suddenly, he grabbed onto my hips and flipped us both over. I shrieked a little. Once he was on top of me, he captured my wrists and held them above my head, much like he'd done when we kissed the night before. I melted into it. As much fun as it had been to feel like I was in charge of him, this was better.

"There we are," he murmured, in between kisses. "That's the Maddy I know."

"I don't know what you mean," I gasped, as he thrust deep inside of me and sent a jolt of sharp pleasure up my spine.

"You don't?" He smiled. "The first time I saw you, I had you pegged for the kind of girl just aching for man to come into her life and order her around." I must have made a face, because he leaned in and chastened me with a quick kiss. "In the bedroom, I mean."

"I…suppose?" I managed. I certainly wasn't going to argue with him, as long as he was making me feel like this.

"Of course you are," he said. "I saw how you reacted just now. I *felt* it. You can't hide the way your body responds to me, Maddy."

I moaned, wrapping my legs around him tightly. I didn't even care what kind of ridiculousness he was spouting. He was filling me up so perfectly, as if our bodies had been expertly molded together.

"Say my name," he murmured, his eyes fixed on mine. They were so dark.

"Daniel," I said.

He shook his head. For all his posturing, though, he was starting to get a little breathless.

"Not that one," he said. "What you used to call me before. When I was your boss."

"Mr. Thorne," I whimpered. "Oh...Mr. Thorne..."

It felt surprisingly good to call him that, after all this time, all this forced intimacy. That was how I thought of him still, sometimes - when I looked at him and remembered - he was my boss. He was my boss, for Christ's sake, a man who'd been essentially a stranger to me until I agreed to marry him. A man who was a stranger still, in many ways, even while he was buried inside me on our honeymoon.

"Mr. Thorne," I whispered. He was smiling. A ripple of pleasure went through my chest.

"Are you close?" he intoned, inches from my ear.

I realized that I was. I nodded.

"Don't," he said. "Not until I say you can."

I stared at him. "I can't...I can't stop it."

"Of course you can." He paused in his movements. "It's simple. If you get too close, just tell me to stop, and I'll stop."

"But I don't want you to stop," I whined, feeling helpless. Why was he playing games with me?

"I don't want to stop either," he replied. "But more than that, I want you to gain control of your body. It won't be hard, if you remember what I taught you. Breathe. Be present."

"Fine." I felt frustrated already, but this was obviously something he got off on. I'd try to play along.

I took a deep breath, and focused. I realized that by concentrating, I could actually control my responses more than I'd realized. I might not understand why he wanted to do this, but it was interesting to know that I could.

I started to relax.

Just then, he slid his hand down to where we were joined.

I shuddered as he caressed me with his fingers. "So I take it I'm allowed now?" I said, shakily.

"No," he said, smilingly. But I could see he was beginning to lose his perfect composure. "Not until I say."

"That's not fair!" I felt like I was seconds away from losing all control.

"I never said I was going to make it easy on you."

I glared at him, but I couldn't keep my eyes open for long. It was like he knew exactly how to touch me. I didn't know how long I could keep this up.

"I don't understand why you're doing this," I gasped.

"You don't?" Sweat was beginning to trickle down the sides of his face. I noticed a muscle in his jaw twitch, and I realized he was actually delaying his own pleasure in order to delay mine. Talk about cutting off your nose to spite your face. What on earth did he get out of this?

"Please, please," I heard myself say. "Please Mr. Thorne, please…"

"Yes," I dimly heard him growl. "Beg."

"Please…please…Mr. Thorne, please…"

"Yes," he said, after what felt like a thousand years. "Yes. Do it. Come for me."

I heard someone yelling hoarsely, and I realized afterwards that it was me. The pleasure swept me up like a hurricane, and when I landed again I felt like I'd traveled a hundred miles. I was spent and panting, and Daniel was trembling on top of me, and I realized he must have finished too.

He rolled off of me, similarly breathless, collapsing on the mattress beside me. Every nerve ending in my body was shuddering with aftershocks. Never - not once in my entire life - had I felt like this.

Okay, so maybe *now* I understood what he got out of it.

"Thank you for…indulging me," he said, after a few moments of silence.

I rolled over onto my side and looked at him. "Is that all it was?"

He kept his eyes on the ceiling. "What do you mean?"

"I mean, this wasn't just some whim, was it?"

He looked mildly uncomfortable with my questioning, but he finally answered. "No. Why, does that bother you?"

"Not at all," I said. "Obviously."

He smiled. "Sometimes people don't really...*like* what they like," he said. "If that makes any sense."

"It does."

I slept much more easily that night, curled up in Daniel's embrace. The next day of astronaut training promised to be more exciting - zero gravity simulations and practice launches, everything we'd need to prepare for the "moon landing" at the end of it. If Sam noticed we were more relaxed and happy around each other, laughing and touching and exchanging little glances more like a real couple, she didn't show any sign of it.

It was great fun. I didn't even get sick in the motion simulators. I could have sworn Daniel was having almost as good of a time as I was, and by the time we got back to the hotel I had almost succeeded in forgetting that he wasn't really my husband.

At dinner, the subject didn't even come up. It was unusual for us to get through an entire conversation without someone even alluding to our arrangement, but we both seemed content to ignore it for now. I wasn't sure if that was a good plan, in the long term. In fact, I knew it wasn't. But just for the honeymoon, I didn't care.

I'd assumed we would be gone for whole week at least, but Daniel told me that three days was the longest he could be away from work. I wasn't too happy about the idea of our time being cut short - especially if it meant things between us were going to change. But there was no use in thinking about that now.

Instead, I focused on what we did have. Even after just a few days, I'd grown used to waking up beside him, seeing him while his eyes were still unfocused and his hair was askew. I'd always thought it was ridiculously corny when people talked about how someone could be more attractive when they were groggy and unkempt, but now, I understood. There was nothing intimidating about him when he'd first woken up - everything from his slightly puffy eyes to his sleepy, crooked smile was downright approachable, and I never thought I'd say that about a man like Mr. Thorne.

On the last day, it was time for my "moon landing." I was strangely giddy about it, maybe because it was something to focus on besides the reality of our honeymoon ending. After a simulated launch and orbit - during which I admittedly did open a bag of Funyuns and then try to catch them all in my mouth - it was time.

They had outfitted a whole room to appear

like the moon's surface, with walls and ceilings speckled with stars, and an image of the earth on one side. The suits we were wearing were heavy and uncomfortable, though certainly not as bad as the real thing. I resisted the urge to quote Neil Armstrong as I stepped out onto the rocky surface.

If I stood there for long enough, I could almost convince myself it was real.

It wasn't, of course - much like my marriage to the man who was currently hopping back towards the lunar lander.

We had to catch a flight early the next morning, but once we got back to the hotel, it was clear that neither one of us felt like sleeping. It started with a smile, on his part - a crooked little number with a secret meaning that I now understood. Next thing I knew he was nibbling on my ear and telling me I'd been bad, which I wasn't sure I had been, but his voice was playful and I didn't really mind in the least.

"Bad girls get spankings," he said, and I cooed.

I stretched out over his lap, arching my back. I'd had boyfriends spank me playfully before, and I'd always found it gave me a pleasant tingle. But I'd always been too shy to ask for more. His hand was warm and strong, and even though it stung, the hits reverberated in my core, turning it molten-hot, making me quiver. I was moaning for him by the time he flipped me over and took me hard and fast, slapping his hand over my mouth when I got too loud.

It was hot, quick, and explosive. I thought that would be it for the night, but a little while later, after we'd ordered a snack from room service, he wanted it again - sweet and slow now, taking our time. When we finally went to sleep, I swear the sky was starting to lighten.

-

The next morning, he was very quiet. We packed slowly, and I didn't bother trying to engage him in conversation. I slept for most of the plane ride, again, and after we got into our taxi back home, I remembered that I wouldn't be going back to my apartment.

Ever.

Strangely, the thought didn't bother me as much as I thought it would.

As much as I'd like to say I was productive for those first few days as Daniel's stay-at-home wife, I spent most of it wandering around aimlessly, watching terrible daytime T.V. and trying to acquaint myself with the place. I unpacked some boxes, and shopped around for art studio supplies online - an easel, maybe? A new desk? A nice chair? I could spend as much as I wanted, and somehow that was more intimidating than liberating. On the third day, when Daniel got home from work, I realized I'd spent the last two hours clicking around the website for one five-hundred-dollar working stool.

He kissed me chastely on the forehead when he walked in, as he always did. We hadn't made love again since coming home, and I hadn't pressed the issue.

"I'm having trouble deciding what to get for my studio," I said.

"Get it all," he said, smiling, just before he stuck his head in the fridge.

"I think we might have a space issue." I walked into the kitchen. "So, how was your day?"

"Fine." He came up for air with a carton of orange juice. "I submitted some forms to the government today, so there's a chance we'll be called for an interview in the next few weeks. Remember what we talked about?"

It felt like a thousand years had passed since then. "Yeah," I said. "I think so. Maybe we should go over some of the details later."

"Of course." He was pouring himself a glass. "I'm not worried. And you shouldn't be either. We'll do just fine."

"Sure," I said. "It's nerve-wracking, though." Not to mention, it was the first time we'd talked about the nature of our arrangement since the honeymoon, and I suppose I wasn't quite prepared for it.

"Well, just try not to think about it for now," he said. "No use borrowing trouble."

"Why'd you bring it up, then?"

"Sorry," he said, grinning. "Greek for dinner?"

"Sure." I sat down on a stool at the breakfast bar. "One of these days I'm going to cook some real food for us."

"Why bother? We've got some of the best restaurants in the country within a twenty-mile radius." He made a dismissive hand gesture as he opened his phone.

"Well, at least it would give me something to do," I muttered.

He set the phone down on the counter and came over to me. "Anything you want to do, you can do it," he said. "You have your car. You have my credit card. Do whatever you want."

"I don't know what I want."

It was true, in more ways than one.

Wisely, he walked away and left me to think. I didn't really want to think, but it was better than trying to talk about it.

I successfully pushed thoughts of the interview into the back of my mind, and the next day I ordered an easel and a light table.

Before long, I had actually set up a studio in the larger of the two spare rooms. We got rid of the bed and superfluous furniture, and the place was roomier than I expected it to be. With the curtains open, the windows even let in a nice amount of natural light.

I started drawing in charcoal again. Slowly, at first, because it had been a while. But before long I had a few rough sketches, and one pretty good drawing of my childhood home. I'd always done still life, mostly. I never liked the challenge of trying to capture the nuance in people's faces.

I came to bed every night when Daniel turned in, but he never touched me beyond a peck on the lips. I wasn't sure if I expected it to change, but I suppose I thought it was worth the shot.

He got the call from the INS a few weeks later.

After he told me, I spent a long time pacing. There was no more drawing in the cards for me. I read everything I could find on the internet about surviving marriage fraud interviews. But none of the write-ups were particularly encouraging, because every single one of them warned me that if I had a sham marriage, there was absolutely no chance I'd be able to convince the INS otherwise.

Well, they probably just said that for legal

reasons.

I hoped.

It took some jumping through hoops to actually schedule the appointment for a time when Daniel could get away from work, but when we finally did, it was a full month away. I didn't know how I was going to survive the anticipation.

I spent a lot more time researching and a lot more time pacing. Daniel pulled out his tiny notebook and we went over everything again, and again and again. He kept telling me that the most important thing was to sound honest and unrehearsed, but I was absolutely sure I was going to make some horribly obvious mistake and ruin everything.

The morning of the interview, I dressed in my most responsible-looking outfit and threw up twice in the bathroom while I was getting ready. The whole drive over, I felt like every organ in my body was trying to crawl out through my chest. I let my hand from my lap down to the seat, where I found Daniel's. I clasped his fingers in mine and squeezed tight, and he squeezed back.

He had, at least, some amount of faith in me. I just wasn't sure if it was justified.

We went to a nondescript building downtown; it could have passed for any other bank of offices. After a long walk down many hallways, we finally arrived at our meeting place.

The waiting room was small, and crowded with people. Most of them had the same thousand-yard stare that I was sure I sported. Not a single one of us wanted to be there. You could practically smell the fear.

I sat there, still clutching Daniel's hand, until his name was called.

"Mr. Thorne?"

I had forgotten they'd be talking to us separately. Of course they would. I let go of his hand and hunched down in my seat.

This was going to be the longest wait of my life.

After a while, I actually started to seriously consider that he might never come back. Maybe they'd already arrested him, and they'd be coming for me next. Of course our story wouldn't hold up. Why would it? We'd been stupid to think we could beat the system.

I sat in utter misery for what felt like hours. Every time the woman came back to the door and looked around the room, my head perked up, hoping against hope it would be my name that she called.

But it never was.

And then, finally, I heard it.

"Mrs. Thorne. Will you please come with me."

I followed her, into a tiny office with barely

enough room for two chairs and a desk. I sat down.

"Someone will be with you in just a moment."

She disappeared.

Sitting there, alone, in the stifling little room, I was very aware of the sound of my own breathing. Did I seem nervous? I had to act normal. I had to remember to smile.

The doorknob rattled.

A middle-aged man walked in, glasses perched on his nose. He was dressed like Mr. Rogers. I smiled bravely at him.

"Mrs. Thorne," he said. "Thank you for coming in."

"My pleasure," I said, absurdly.

"All right." He opened a manila folder on his desk. "Let's get started, shall we?"

Chapter Thirteen

I sat quietly, irrationally worried that the interviewer could hear my heartbeat. The silence seemed to stretch on forever, and then, he finally spoke.

"Can you tell me about your first meeting?"

I cleared my throat. "Well, uh, he runs the company that I work at. But he doesn't take a very...hands-on role in dealing with his staff. So I saw him around for years before I ever really 'met' him." I inhaled, slowly. Breathing. Staying present with myself. "Then, about three months ago, he sent his lawyer to get me. He told me that Daniel wanted to meet with me."

"And what happened then?"

"Daniel wanted to talk about a special project. A logo redesign for the company. Complete image overhaul. He wanted to keep it a secret, which was why he was talking to me about it directly. Or so he said."

"It wasn't true?"

I smiled. "He made it all up, just to get a chance to talk to me. I guess he'd been, sort of...interested in me for a while."

"Did he make you aware of his interest in the first meeting?"

I swallowed. We hadn't gone over this. "Not...not in so many words."

The interviewer looked at me, clicking his pen.

"I...suspected," I said, at last. "From the way he looked at me. But I thought I must be imagining things."

"So." He looked down at his papers. "Where were you living, at this time?"

I recited the address to my old apartment.

"At your first meeting, did you exchange contact information? Did you make arrangements to see each other again?"

I hesitated. "I...I think so," I said. "But I can't really remember exactly how many times we met before he gave me his number."

So far, I was following Daniel's guidelines as closely as I could. I figured vague was best, but too vague and I risked looking suspicious. I had to walk a delicate balance.

And breathe.

"Can you tell me about when you first realized you had something in common?"

I laughed a little, looking into the distance, like I was remembering something that made me happy to think about. "I don't remember how it came up, exactly, but...Woody Allen movies. Turns out we both grew up watching them. We started talking about them every time we got together, just chit-chatting...less and less about the 'project,' and more and more about personal things. Finally, he told me that they were putting the project on hold, but...he still wanted to see me."

"And you felt the same way."

"Yes."

A part of me was actually starting to believe my own story, and it made my heart ache.

"So would you say that's when your relationship turned romantic?"

I nodded.

"Where did you go on your first date?"

"We ate lunch together at the office quite a bit," I said. "But...officially? The Inn at Grenarnia," I said. "It was very nice."

"Do you remember the date?"

"I think it was...around the end of July?

"Were you concerned about your co-workers finding out about your relationship?"

"We were, for a while. That's why we kept it quiet. But eventually we decided it was best to be open about things, and that I would quit my job as soon as it was feasible to avoid conflicts of interest."

"How soon into the relationship did he inform you about his immigration difficulties?"

"Before he proposed," I said. "He wanted to make sure I knew that it wasn't about that."

"And when was that?"

I looked down. "After a few weeks of dating for real," I said. "He told me that he knew it was crazy...but the craziest part was, I felt exactly the same way. I was ready to take a leap of faith."

"What made you decide to have a short engagement?"

"Well, neither one of us is particularly romantic. I didn't want a big fuss and he didn't either. So we figured there was no reason to let things drag out forever."

"How did your parents feel about the relationship?"

I hesitated for a moment. "My parents and I aren't...close. I invited them to the wedding, but they wouldn't travel. Daniel's parents have passed away."

"Well, that takes care of my next question." The interviewer looked up, smiling a little bit. Finally showing his human side.

I just kept breathing.

More questions came after that. About the wedding, the number of people in attendance, about who took care of the finances and what T.V. shows we watched together every week. He asked to see my keys, examining the one I said was for Daniel's apartment. I wondered if he was trying to match them up from memory.

He wanted to know if I'd met any members of Daniel's family, so I told him about Lindsey and Ray. I answered a long string of mundane questions about our home life - the number of bedrooms and bathrooms, when the garbage pickup came, and the color of the carpet.

Finally, he released me. I walked back out into the waiting room slowly. Daniel jumped up out of his chair when he spotted me.

I hurried over to him; he pulled me close and kissed me swiftly.

"We survived," I said.

"Yes." He put his arm around my shoulders. "Come on. Let's go."

I had to bite my tongue until we got back

home, although I was dying to compare whatever answers we could remember. John was driving, and he didn't know the truth.

As soon as the door closed behind us, I turned to him and blurted out:

"Did they ask you if you came onto me at our first meeting?"

He blinked. "I said that I was flirting with you, but being subtle about it. What did you say?"

I exhaled. "I said that I thought maybe you were, but I wasn't sure."

"That's fine, then." He pressed a quick kiss to my forehead. "I'm sure everything will match perfectly. There's really nothing to worry about."

"When will we find out?"

"I should get a letter in a few months," he said. "If we don't hear anything between now and then, we're to assume everything's going smoothly. Which I'm sure it will."

"I'm glad you're so confident."

"Come on." He laid his hands on my shoulders. "It's all right. I know this isn't the easiest thing in the world, with all the waiting, but everything will be just fine."

I smiled, and then looked away for a moment. I wanted, very badly, to say something about the honeymoon. About the fact that we hadn't really touched each other since. About the fact that I wanted, more than anything, for him to grab me and take me like I knew he really wanted to.

I *knew* he did, even if he wasn't showing it.

"We had a good time on the honeymoon," I said, finally. "Didn't we?"

"Yes," he said, a little hesitantly.

"And I'm not talking about the moon walk."

His mouth twitched.

"Maddy," he said. "Maybe we shouldn't -"

"What - talk about it?" I touched the side of his face. "*Do* it? What difference does it make?"

He swallowed. "Maddy," he said, a little hoarsely. So I was getting to him, at least.

"We're going to feel what we feel," I said. "Whether we act on it or not."

He licked his lips. "All the same," he said.

"All the same? What kind of counter-argument is that?" I smiled. "Stop acting like a character in some Victorian loss-of-virtue novel."

He laughed, and then leaned down to kiss me. "You're very persuasive, you know that?" he said when he broke away. "That's very naughty. Tempting me. You know I can't resist."

"Why would I ever want you to?" I wound my arms around his neck, smiling.

"I don't know if you realize what you've unleashed." He had such a wicked grin on his face. "Go upstairs and wait for me."

I frowned a little. "Why?"

"Because I said so."

He was still smiling.

"Fine," I said. "But you better make it worth my while." I turned and skipped up the stairs, two at a time.

"Oh, I will," he shouted after me.

I stood in the middle of the bedroom for a moment, trying to decide how to present myself. The obvious thing would be to undress completely - or at least partway. But he'd be expecting that. He wanted to punish me, didn't he? And strangely enough, I wanted to be punished too. So I should be bad, right? I should do the opposite of what he expected. What he wanted.

I went over to the small bookshelf by the door. I hadn't looked at it too much; it was mostly business stuff or financial guides, nothing that really interested me. But there were a few novels on the top shelf, so I picked one at random and sat down on the edge of the bed. It looked like something you'd buy at the airport on a whim. I flipped it open and started reading.

Minutes ticked by, and I hadn't turned the page. I couldn't really process the words. I felt nervous and excited, my heart thumping wildly in my chest, more so even than it had at the interview.

Suddenly, I heard a light tapping noise. I looked up.

Daniel was standing in the doorway, leaning against the frame, his fingers drumming out a staccato on the smoothly painted wood. He was smiling, coldly.

"I thought I told you to wait for me."

"I *am* waiting," I said, innocently. I looked up, setting the book down on the mattress. "I got bored. Is that a crime?"

He strode over rapidly, stopping a few feet away from me and staring down at me. I swore his eye twitched.

"When I tell you wait for me," he said, his voice low and dangerous, "you *wait* for me. You don't read. You don't check your phone. You don't think. You just wait. That's all you are allowed to do."

My throat tightened. He was right - I had no idea what I'd unleashed. This was a side of him I hadn't seen before. It was a strange, intimate version of his forbidding work persona, more like how I'd imagined he would be in private. And apparently, I was right. I just hadn't known how right, until now.

I'd intended to keep up the defiant act for a little longer, but I found the words stuck in my throat.

"I'm...I'm sorry," I said. "I didn't know."

"Well, you should have." He walked over to his closet and began rifling through his belt rack. I felt all the blood drain from my face. Was he really going to do what I thought he was going to do?

A little spanking was one thing, but I wasn't sure I was ready to get hit with a belt.

Then again, there was something inside me - something that stopped me from protesting. A very small voice, but very clear.

I trusted him.

He came back with a belt looped in his hand. I was afraid, yet at the same time, I wasn't.

"What do you think?" he said. "Is this what you deserve?"

I swallowed. "No," I said, very quietly.

He smiled. "Maybe not," he said, looking down at the leather in his hand. He loosened his grip and let it slither to the floor.

"Maybe this would be more appropriate," he said, reaching for the book.

"Thank God I picked a paperback," I said, before I could stop myself.

He grabbed me by my arm, flipping me over onto my stomach. I squealed.

"You've got a smart tongue," he said. "You really should learn to control it a little better."

He spanked me with the book. Hard. It didn't sting as badly as I thought it would, especially through my jeans, but it was a powerful swing. I groaned into the pillow, half out of pain and half out of pleasure.

He was relentless, but at the same time, I could tell he was paying attention to me. Gauging my body's reactions. He wasn't going to give me more than I could take.

Just when I was beginning to grow numb, I heard him toss the book aside.

"Turn over," he said.

I did.

His smile was gentler now, and he leaned down to kiss me.

"This is all just a silly game," he whispered. "You know that, right?"

I nodded.

"If you say stop I'll stop," he said. "It ends. No questions, no hesitations."

"I know." I took a deep breath. "I trust you."

"Good," he said. His face changed. "Now, get yourself undressed." He stood up, stepping away from the bed to watch me. I met his eyes as I pulled my shirt off over my head.

"Slowly," he said.

I raised an eyebrow, sliding down off the bed with what I hoped was a smooth, sensual movement and unbuttoning my jeans. I made a show of shimmying out of them, dragging it out for much longer than I needed to. I tossed them aside, and then started on the bra, making sure my hair fell down over my ear in a very fetching way as I did so. I unclasped it, hook by hook, until it was finally undone. Then, I let it fall to the floor.

One piece left.

I hooked my thumbs in the waistband of my panties, just above my hips. I slid them down, inch by inch, making sure to turn around and give him the three hundred and sixty-five degree view.

Finally, I was naked in front of him in his own bedroom. It felt different than it had on the honeymoon. More real. He came walking towards me.

"Shameless," he said, grabbing me by my wrists and pulling me towards him, slightly off-balance. I stumbled into his body, and made no effort to recover myself. Not that I could have, even if I'd wanted to. He was holding me far too tightly.

He made a small noise with his tongue: *tsk, tsk*. But he couldn't stop himself from smiling.

"Wait here," he said, and I stood there by the bed while he went into his closet and rummaged for a moment. I don't know what I was expecting him to bring out, but it certainly wasn't a length of rope. It was long and elegant, and it had been dyed a deep wine-red. He let it slide across my skin, and I shivered at the silken feel of it.

"I ought to tie you up and just leave you

here," he whispered.

I swear my heart stopped for a moment.

"But that wouldn't be very much fun for me, would it?" he finished, and I breathed again.

He looped the rope around my wrists first, lightly; testing me. I relaxed into it, and he drew the ends tighter. Going strictly by feel, it was hard to tell exactly what he was doing, but at the end of it, my arms were bound together tightly. I could lift them a little, but they were so well attached at the wrist that I could do little else.

The rope felt stiff, like it was brand new. Had he bought it just for me, or had his last relationship exploded spectacularly before he had a chance to tie her up? Somehow, I didn't picture any romantic entanglement of his could possibly end well.

This hadn't been something I had fantasized about - not really. But I could see the appeal. There was a momentary panic when I first realized how immobilized I really was, how vulnerable, but I soon came to peace with it. And that feeling of calm overtook me completely, surrounding me like a warm blanket. Freed from the obligation of movement, all I could do was wait for him to touch me. Which, really, was all I *wanted* to do.

I stood there patiently, focusing on my breathing just like he'd taught me to do.

"Kneel on the bed," was the next thing he said to me.

I clambered up on the mattress - awkwardly, without the use of my arms for balance - and waited there for him. I felt him kneel behind me, resting his hand on my shoulder and pushing, gently. I lost my balance completely and pitched face-first into the pillows. I managed to arrange myself so I could breathe, but I couldn't really see him and I wasn't sure I could get myself upright again without his help.

His hand rested on my ass. I had done such a good job focusing on my breathing until now that it was only just occurring to me what a vulnerable position I was in. On my knees, with my face in the pillows - he could see everything. I was pretty sure I'd never been this exposed to anyone before. I could feel the anxiety beginning to creep in. I exhaled, slowly.

Daniel was running his finger up the inside of my thigh. "You're so beautiful," he murmured, almost to himself, and I had a hysterical urge to laugh. What a strange thing to say, in a moment like this. It was almost like he meant it.

A moment later I heard a wrapper tear, and then I felt him pressing against me, sliding in easily until he was buried to the hilt. I groaned softly against the pillow. He felt perfect inside me - he always had. With every movement, I felt him deep inside - in the very obvious, literal sense, but also in a different way, that made my heart swell in my chest. Oh, no. This *was* dangerous. But not in the way I'd expected it to be.

I never would have guessed that a simple length of rope could wreak such havoc on my psyche. As much as I'd enjoyed our previous encounters, this was something completely different. It felt so much more intimate, in a way I hadn't expected. Every little sensation, from the bruising grip of his fingers on my hips to the soft brush of the pillowcase against my cheek, was making my skin tingle all over. My shoulders were starting to hurt, but it was a dull, satisfying ache. It felt *good*.

He hit a spot deep inside me that made me shudder, and I felt warm tendrils of pleasure creeping through my whole body. Its peak was somehow both gradual and sudden - like watching a water balloon explode in slow motion. I made soft, muffled noises as my body pulsed and shivered. In the midst of it I felt him swell inside of me, his hips finally stilling their incessant movements.

He pulled away from me then, coming back moments later to coax me onto my side and quickly undo the ropes. I felt completely blissed-out and exhausted, overwhelmed, like I might start laughing and crying and not be able to stop for hours. He slung his arm around me and I curled up against him, the warmth of his skin and the sound of his heartbeat somehow reaching me through the haze of feelings and sensations to still my mind.

I breathed.

Chapter Fourteen

The next morning, I came down to the kitchen with a smile on my face. Daniel returned my "good morning" somewhat distractedly - I wasn't sure what I expected him to say, but it certainly wasn't the next thing that came out of his mouth.

"Last night," he said. "That can't...we can't let that happen again."

"What do you mean?" I knew exactly what he meant, but I didn't want to believe it.

"We can't blur the boundaries," he said. "We're in a business arrangement. It's not very...it's a bad idea to let things get so muddled."

"I thought you agreed that it didn't matter."

His eyes looked sad, but determined. I knew I wasn't going to really talk him out of this, but I wouldn't be able to forgive myself if I didn't try.

"Maddy, I'm sorry. I know it's been fun. It's not personal. You're very lovely. I have a good time when we're...together. But it can't keep happening. We have to control ourselves."

I wanted to scream.

I wanted to fight him, to bite and kick, throw things at him - I wanted to do every irrational thing that came to my mind, but instead I just stood there, very still, staring at him. Nodding.

He watched me for a moment, waiting for the other shoe to drop. But I wouldn't give him the satisfaction.

"Okay," I said, in the most neutral voice I could manage.

I turned and disappeared into my studio, where I proceeded to scribble so hard into a new pad of paper that I tore through five sheets before I stopped.

-

After that, things were very quiet. We rarely spoke, dodging each other in the main rooms and sleeping three feet apart. Thank God for that massive bed. I was beginning to think that things would just stay like this forever - well, not forever. For the remainder of the year, at any rate.

I learned to dread the weekends. Things weren't so bad when I was alone, but I couldn't even focus on my art when I knew he was in the apartment. Thankfully, he started to spend more and more time away from home, even when he wasn't working. I never asked where he was. Sometimes, he wasn't even home by the time I went to bed.

One Monday morning, I came downstairs to find that he was still in the kitchen. Shit. It was a holiday. I'd completely forgotten. I tried to look away and walk past him to the fridge, but I could feel his eyes on me and I knew he was about to say something.

He said, very deliberately and coldly: "Would it be too much of a burden for you to wash the dishes that you use?"

I slammed the fridge closed. "Are you referring to the *single bowl* I left in the sink last night?"

"And the glasses the night before, and the plates before that..." He set down his coffee mug very deliberately. "It's always something. I don't think it's unreasonable of me to expect-"

"They had to soak!" I glared at him.

"They wouldn't have to," he said, "if you'd just wash them as soon as you use them."

"Oh my God. I can't believe we're having this conversation."

He sighed. "I'm just trying to make it a little easier for us to live together."

"No, you're trying to make it easier for *you* to live with *me*."

"You're more than welcome to let me know

if there's anything I can do to make your life easier," he said, in the flattest tone possible.

"Oh, yeah?" I stepped closer to him. "I'm so glad you raised that subject. How about treating me like a human being? And not trying to act like nothing ever happened between us?"

He looked at me balefully. "Do you really want to have this conversation again?"

"Yes," I said. "I really would. Because I'd like to know what the hell's wrong with you."

"What the hell is wrong with *you*?" he demanded. He stood up, a muscle in his jaw twitching. "Do you not understand what's happening here? Do you not see how *hard* this is?" For a moment, he looked crazed, his eyes darting from side to side as he searched for the right words. "Being near you, all the time...seeing you all the time...*sleeping* next to you...God damn it, Maddy. Are you really that self-absorbed? Are you really that *selfish*?"

I recoiled. His words stung; I wanted to insist that I didn't know what he was talking about, but of course I did.

"I'm so sorry," I said, at last, very quietly. I could hear my voice shaking. "I didn't realize that I was twisting your arm." I felt furious, but to my utter humiliation, it was expressing itself in the form of hot tears leaking out of the corners of my eyes and sliding down my face.

"That's not what I said." Daniel looked

utterly defeated, slumping back down on one of the bar stools. "You *know* that's not what I said."

"No, I'm sorry, you just said I was selfish. And self-absorbed." My voice was thick from crying, and I hated the sound of it. "That's a whole lot better."

"I'm sorry," he said, not sounding particularly apologetic. "But you know what I mean."

"Yeah, sure. Fine." I was done with this whole conversation - I wasn't going to stand there and stare at his stupid unreadable expression while I blubbered like a stupid baby. It was humiliating. I turned to go upstairs, and to my mortification, he followed me.

"Can you just leave me alone?" I didn't sound quite as authoritative as I'd hoped, between sniffles.

"Not until you agree to stop toying with me," he said, flatly.

Wait a minute - *I* was toying with *him*? Okay, that was rich.

"Sure," I said, dripping sarcasm. "I'll make sure to get right on that." I opened the top drawer of the bureau, rifling through it for something - anything - just to look busy so I didn't have to make eye contact with him.

"I mean it, Maddy," he said. "We can't keep doing this. *I* can't keep doing this."

I whirled on him, with a handful of jewelry clutched in my fist. I had no idea what I was even in my jewelry box in the first place. "Okay, fine! Fuck!" I shouted. "I'll leave you the hell alone! As God is my witness, I'll never shimmy my ass in front of you again!"

He winced, a little. Good. "I'm sorry," he said, again. This time he sounded like he might mean it, a little. "If I led you on."

Oh, good, the classic "if" apology. Hardly an apology at all. I could feel my lip curling up into an actual snarl; I couldn't remember ever feeling this angry in my life.

"Oh, you mean the incredibly thoughtful honeymoon?" My tone was venomous. I hardly recognized my own voice. "All those little presents? The car, the clothes, all that shit? Everything you'd give to a woman you actually loved? Well, you can keep them, Danny. I don't give a shit!"

I hurled whatever was in my hand in his general direction. He dodged, and something winged his ear; when they hit the opposite wall I realized it was one of the very first things he'd bought for me - the necklace and earrings to go with my blue dress, the ones I'd loved so much, now sitting in a heap on the carpet.

The buzzer went off downstairs.

"Christ," Daniel muttered, walking over to the stairs, rubbing his ear. I followed, halfheartedly. The sudden shift had taken away all of my momentum, and I barely felt like fighting anymore. I stayed off to the side, however, not particularly wanting to be seen in my current state.

Daniel opened the door.

"Mr. Thorne?"

The voice sounded vaguely familiar - and for some reason, it made my heart drop into my stomach.

There was a silence.

"Yes," he said, testily.

"It's Jordan Camry," said the voice. "From the INS. May I come in?"

I wanted to turn and run, but I felt like my feet were glued to the floor. So I just stood there, staring dumbly, as the same man who'd quizzed me about our relationship strode into the hallway, like he had some right to.

He glanced at me, nodding politely. "Mrs. Thorne," he said, not reacting - not visibly, anyway - to my tear-streaked face.

"Is this about the interview?" Daniel said, finally finding his voice.

Mr. Camry looked at him. "No," he said, at last. "But concerns have been raised about the validity of your marriage. In such cases, an unscheduled home visit is customary. Of course, you have the right of refusal. But if you do refuse, other measures will be taken."

"No," said Daniel. "We - that's fine. You can...do whatever you need to do."

"Can one of you show me around the different rooms of the house?" he asked.

Daniel nodded, coming forward. They went to the guest rooms first, including my studio - thank God I *was* sleeping in Daniel's bed - while my husband prattled on mechanically about each stop. Mr. Camry nodded, taking notes. They disappeared upstairs for a while, and then came back down.

"Thank you," Mr. Camry said, shaking Daniel's hand. "I appreciate your cooperation. I'll be sure to make a note of it in the report."

He walked out the door, and I exhaled. I realized he must have only been here for a few minutes, but it had felt like hours.

"What in the *fuck*," I said, as Daniel turned towards me, his eyes furious. But not at me, this time.

"Someone must have said something." He clenched and unclenched his fists. "Someone must have contacted them. They don't do this for just anyone."

We wandered over to the living room, single-mindedly, both sitting down on the sofa with our minds racing.

"Lisa," I blurted out. I'd hardly spared my *actual* boss a thought since she'd gone on maternity leave - out of sight, out of mind definitely applied when I had so many other things to worry about - but she'd been the one to recommend me as a green card bride in the first place. "You said she's one of the only people who knows."

He shook his head before I'd even finished speaking. "She would never," he said, firmly. That was clearly the end of that discussion. Oh, well. If he didn't want to consider the possibility, I certainly wasn't going to change his mind.

My mind kept on racing, thinking of every person in the office who might have reason to be suspicious. As far as motive, I wasn't sure. Did the INS offer some kind of incentive? Or would they have turned us in for purely personal reasons?

Wait a minute. His secretary, with the dagger eyes.

"Alice," I said.

He turned to look at me, frowning. "Alice is a professional," he said. "Besides, she doesn't know."

"She might suspect," I said. "She might have overheard something - right?"

"Even if she did. Why would she go to all the trouble of reporting us?"

"Have you seen the way she looks at me?" I looked down at my lap. "She *hates* me."

"She doesn't hate you," Daniel insisted.

"Don't be ridiculous."

"I'm not being ridiculous!" I insisted, jumping to my feet almost without realizing it, and pacing around the room. "She looks like she wants to kill me."

"She'd never do that," he said. "You have to trust my judgment, Maddy."

"Why? Who says you're infallible?"

"No one. But I choose my intimates very carefully. No one close to me would have betrayed my confidence. I'm sure about that."

I turned to glare at him. "So you're saying it has to be someone *I* know."

"I didn't say that." He raised his hands, palms outward. "Did I say that?"

"You don't have to." I stood in front of him, arms crossed. "Just so you know, I've never said a word to anybody. I'm the loneliest person I know, because I can't be honest with anyone."

"Do you think I *like* lying to my sister?" Daniel snapped. "Get down off your cross. You didn't have any friends before we got married, either. You can't pin that one on me."

I fumed silently for a moment.

"I'm sorry," he said, at last. "Maddy, I'm sorry. I shouldn't have said that. But we both have to calm down. This is getting us nowhere."

"Fine," I muttered, sitting back down. "Alice seems like a no-brainer, though, I'm sorry."

"Trust me," he said, "she's been working for

me long enough. I know she's abrasive, but I also know what she's not capable of. And a large-scale betrayal like this is beyond her, even if she found out about us."

"All right. Fine." I breathed out, slowly. But I didn't feel any calmer. "Who else might have suspected? If we're eliminating all the people who actually know..."

"It could be anyone, really," he said. "Anyone from the office might have looked at us and decided we seemed suspicious...who the hell knows, really. We both have a guilty conscience. I have no idea how something might have appeared to someone on the outside of the situation. God, what a nightmare." He stopped, resting his head in his hands and raking his fingers through his hair. I knew how he felt. I was crawling out of my skin.

There was absolutely nothing I could say or do to comfort him, or myself. We both spent the rest of the afternoon absently Googling various things related to our predicament and wandering around the apartment, picking things up and putting them down again in random places. I sat in front of a blank sheet of paper for a while, charcoal in hand, but nothing came to me.

Late in the afternoon, the buzzer went off again. I don't know why, but my heart leapt into my throat. Daniel hurried to answer it.

Someone was delivering a package of some kind. I walked over, slowly, fists clenched.

Somehow, I knew, even before he looked up at me and I saw the hunted look in his eyes.

"What is it?" I reached out, and although he didn't extend it to me, he didn't try to pull it away.

It had come in a certified mail envelope. It was a single sheet of paper, typewritten.

I took it.

I'm sorry. I did what I did in anger, and I shouldn't have done it, but it can't be undone now.

I told the immigration people what you did.

You can imagine how I felt when I heard you were going out with her, of all people. I didn't think it through, I just wanted to lash out, and I wish I hadn't. When I found out it was fake, I couldn't believe my luck at first, and I acted on my first instinct. It was a terrible idea. I'm sorry.

I don't know if they will have contacted you by now, so I'm not sure if this is a warning, or just an apology. I hope that you can convince them I lied about you two. It shouldn't be too hard. I'm sure I'll get in trouble, but I'm not sure that I care anymore.

If you're wondering how I knew, you might want to consult Mr. Wegman. He's got a weakness for blondes, and he doesn't lock up his papers very carefully at night when he's been drinking. If I were you, I'd find a new lawyer.

I'm so sorry, darling. I couldn't help it.

All my love,
Flo

"*Florence?*" I said, disbelieving. I looked up at him.

His face said everything I really needed to know.

"We were…" he hesitated for a long moment. "…involved…years ago. The breakup wasn't…it was ugly. Neither one of us conducted ourselves well, I think. When she came to me later looking for work, I had my second thoughts of course…but I felt bad for how I'd treated her during that time; how could I turn her down when she needed my help?" He squeezed his eyes shut, still processing the whole thing. "And I suppose…I suppose…" His eyes flew open. "Christ. Wegman. I have to go over there - I have to make him burn the contract. Immediately. I have to…"

"Please don't kill him," I said, only half in jest.

"You think I want to add murder one to my already considerable list of crimes?" He grabbed his jacket and keys. "Don't go anywhere."

"Why would I?"

"I don't know. Just - don't."

Alone with my thoughts after he slammed

the door behind him, I tried to imagine what kind of bitterness would lead someone to do what Florence did. I never would have counted her among my close friends, but it was still a shock to the system that she had the capacity to do something like that.

I lay on the sofa, staring at the ceiling, until Daniel got home. He looked exhausted. He threw his keys on the table and came over to the sofa, collapsing next to my feet.

"I'm sorry I never told you," he said. "About me and Flo. I didn't think it would matter."

"You couldn't have known," I said. I wasn't angry with him. Why should I expect him to tell me that he'd once dated her? What difference did it make? It wasn't like we were in a relationship, or anything crazy like that.

I felt gnawed-out and empty inside. All my life, I'd run up against little stumbling blocks - annoyances, really - small things that felt much bigger at the time, but were ultimately solvable, more or less. But this was different. I'd never grappled with a problem that was truly bigger than I was. This was no overdue utility payment or busted transmission. This was a potential felony charge, this was five years in prison. This was my life, changed forever. And not in the way I'd signed on for.

In retrospect, of course, it seemed insane that I had ever agreed to this arrangement.

Even as careful as we'd been - all the effort we'd gone to, trying to make sure we seemed legitimate - all it took was one careless slip by his lawyer and a vengeful ex. Something neither one of us could have seen coming, not from a million miles away.

We went to bed late that night, and I don't think either of us slept at all. I went about my day mechanically, not really aware of what I was actually doing, and Daniel came home from work early just to sit on the sofa and stare off into space, with a slight frown on his face.

Things went on like that for days - we barely spoke, except to re-hash the same conversations over and over again, *how could this have happened, can you believe it, what's going to happen if...*

Daniel had dark circles under his eyes, growing darker every day. I was sure I didn't look any better, but I hardly left the house, so it didn't matter.

I couldn't remember the last time I'd felt this awful. It was the sort of stress that wears away at you slowly, the kind that rarely spikes to panic proportions, but that sits quietly, draining your energy with every heartbeat, until you can hardly keep your eyes open - but of course, you can't sleep. It's ever-present, murmuring awful thoughts in your ear, until it commands nearly all of your attention. You want nothing more than to ignore it, but you can't.

One morning, after weeks of this, I went to fetch the mail as I always did. In spite of everything, I still felt a spike of mixed fear and anticipation every time I unlocked the box - I don't know what I expected to find.

But today, I found it.

There was an envelope from the INS. I opened it with shaking hands, my vision going black around the edges as I struggled to focus on the words.

Dear Mr. Thorne,

Your application for permanent residency has been processed and accepted...

I fumbled with my phone, barely having the presence of mind to rush back to the apartment before I called so I wasn't babbling about the INS and residency applications in front of God and everyone.

He answered just as I slammed the front door behind me.

"There's a letter," I blurted out, "it says they accepted your application. Does that mean...?"

He was silent for a moment. "I think so," he said. "I think...I think so."

"Congratulations," I said.

"I'm coming home early. I need to arrange some things. And I'd like to see it."

"Of course," I said.

"Right. See you in a minute."

I sat down, heavily, on the sofa. So this was it. This was what it had all been for. Why did I feel like punching a hole in the goddamn wall?

Chapter Fifteen

When Daniel walked through the door, he didn't say a word to me - didn't even shed his laptop bag and coat at the door. He just walked straight over to me with his hand outstretched, and I held out the letter obediently. His eyes scanned all over it, quickly, from top to bottom and then once more.

"Well," he said, setting it down on the coffee table.

"Well," I agreed.

He finally lifted the strap of the bag over his head, setting it down on the floor, and stripped out of his coat. He sat down next to me and stared at his hands for a moment.

"I've been consulting with some people," he said. "My new lawyer - chosen very carefully, I promise. I don't think she'll have quite as much of a weakness for Flo as Wegman did. And I talked to some people on the inside who are pulling for me. They've all agreed that we're through the woods now. There'll be no more interviews or surprise visits. The decision's been made, the file's been sealed. So really - there's no reason to keep doing this."

I stared at him. "Sorry?"

"I know what the contract says." He met my eyes, finally. I couldn't quite read his face. "Six more months. But I'm willing to break it, if you are. I can have the money by tomorrow."

I clasped my fingers together tightly in my lap. "I think that's a little premature. I promise I'll stop throwing things at your head."

He let out a little huff of laughter. "Regardless," he said. "I think this will be better for both of us. Don't you?"

I bit my lip. "I always just...I guess I just figured we'd stick to the terms of our agreement."

"I did too. But wouldn't you rather go home?"

"I'm not sure what you want me to say."

"I'm sorry," he said, after a moment's hesitation. "I thought this would be an easy decision for you. I wouldn't have brought it up, otherwise."

"I just don't think it's a good idea to assume we're out of the woods," I said. "Do you?"

He was tapping out an abstract rhythm on his knee, his fingers seeming to move almost of their own accord. "Please don't take this the wrong way," he said, finally. "But I really do think it'll be better if we don't have to see each other."

My throat felt very dry. "Better for who?" I said.

He didn't answer - he just stood and walked away, up the stairs to the bedroom, shutting the door behind him. It seemed our fight wasn't over.

He was right. I had to remind myself of that, forcefully, because I felt like I'd been punched in the stomach. We were getting entangled with each other in a way that simply wasn't practical. Proximity had fooled us into believing we were...if not in love, then at least some reasonable facsimile of it.

Sitting there alone on the sofa, I remembered a beginning psychology class I'd taken in college, because it seemed like the easiest way to fulfill a science requirement. The professor had gone around the room and asked everyone to name the place where they'd encountered their last romantic interest - a chorus of *school, work, school, work, school, school, and work* followed. The teacher explained that people feel more affection and emotional investment with people to whom they are close in proximity. We don't date classmates and co-workers just because it's convenient, we do it because we are literally *close* to them.

I'd been so, so stupid to think I could live with a man who looked like Daniel and not find myself head-over-heels for him within a few months. No matter what I "knew," the deeper parts of my brain - the parts I couldn't control - would whisper sweet nothings until I lost myself in feelings that didn't make any logical sense at all.

A man like Daniel had no time for someone like me. He'd made that abundantly clear.

Finally, I managed to drag myself up off the sofa and over to my studio, in the spare bedroom. I folded up my easel and packed up all my charcoals and pastels, getting everything ready for a move to...

...where the hell would I go?

This whole time, I'd been picturing myself going back to my old apartment. But of course, that wasn't "my apartment" anymore. Someone else lived there now. I hadn't expected to grapple with this question so soon, and now I was completely lost. Where on earth would I go? And I had to consider that quite literally. With two million dollars, I could go anywhere I wanted and start an entirely new life.

Daniel had left his laptop bag sitting in the living room where he'd dropped it, so I pulled out the computer and started to browse. After a few minutes, in spite of myself, I found myself back to browsing apartments that were ten minutes away. I didn't particularly love this city, but at least it was familiar.

There was something to be said for familiarity.

When Daniel finally emerged from the bedroom, I half-expected him to have packed all my clothes into liquor boxes. He hadn't, of course. I wondered if he expected *me* to do it.

Which reminded me - I was going to need some boxes.

While he stood in front of the open fridge, staring, as if he expected some previous unknown foodstuffs to have appeared in the last few hours, I heard his phone go off in his pocket. I made the barest effort to pretend I wasn't listening, but of course I was.

"Lindsey," he said, turning to look at me. "Hi."

I perked up.

"You're going to be in town this weekend? Well, that's great news. Just you?"

I watched his face carefully, but he betrayed almost nothing.

"Of course you can stay here," he said. "Maddy can move her art supplies out of the big spare room....no, no, don't worry about it, it's no problem."

After they'd finalized their plans and said their goodbyes, I stood up and headed into the kitchen. Daniel shoved the phone back in his pocket.

"Well," he said. "I guess we'd better delay things until she's gone home, at least."

"See," I said. "This is the kind of thing I'm talking about."

He shrugged. "If you'd already moved out, I just would have told her you were away at an...art conference." He pulled a beer out of the fridge. "That's a thing that exists, isn't it?"

"With all my clothes and personal belongings?" I countered.

"And the place is being sprayed for cockroaches, so she can't come over."

"Sure, there's no *way* she'll get suspicious."

"We can talk about this after she leaves," he said, meaningfully, prying the lid off his beer and tossing it into the trash can. From his tone, it was quite clear he wasn't really open to further negotiations.

Well. We'd see about that.

-

Lindsey arrived on Friday evening, all smiles and sass like usual. She hugged me tightly, then promptly took us out to a late dinner and bought us enough drinks that we were actually able to act like a couple again.

Daniel retired to bed early, leaving me and Lindsey sitting on the sofa, quietly chit-chatting about everything that came to mind. She'd managed to land another big client who was even more insufferable than the last, so we chuckled over her stories for a while as the clock ticked quietly in the background.

After a silence, she switched gears.

"Is everything going okay between you two?"

I hesitated. Obviously, we weren't pretending as well as I'd thought. "I guess so," I said, although nothing could be further from the truth. "It's just tough right now. I'm not really sure why."

"Danny tends to bring his work stress home with him," Lindsey said, stretching her legs out in front of her. "He has trouble letting it go. I'm sure that's not easy for you."

"Yeah," I said, vaguely, hugging my knees to my chest. The urge to be honest with her was almost overwhelming me. It was welling up in my throat. But I couldn't. I knew I couldn't.

"Hey, are you hungry?" Lindsey glanced up at the clock. "Jesus. It's been ages since dinner. No wonder. I think I'm going to order a pizza, you want any?"

"Sure, I guess. Any kind. I'm not picky." I played with a loose thread on my shirt while Lindsey made her phone call. I was trying to think of a way I could get advice from her without actually being honest about what was going on. The opportunity to get her unique perspective on Daniel's behavior was just too tempting.

When she sat back down, I had something prepared.

"Do you ever feel like Daniel's sort of...distant?"

"Oh, all the time," Lindsey replied. "He's just trying to protect himself - I don't know why, but I always figured he let his guard down around you."

"Maybe not as much as I thought," I admitted. "Sometimes it's like I just can't read him. I have no idea what he wants from me."

Lindsey was nodding, slowly. "It's not easy," she said. "I wish I had a simple answer for you, but even I can't get him to open up, most of the time. He has to get there on his own. Most people do, really." She looked off into the distance, thoughtfully. "He's a tough nut to crack, that one."

The buzzer went off.

"Well, that was fast," Lindsey said, getting to her feet. "Somebody's getting an extra good tip."

She flung the door open.

A voice came into the room from the hallway:

"*Where is he*?"

My heart dropped into my stomach.

Florence stormed into the room, unkempt

and rain-drenched, dripping all over the floor. I must have stared at her like a deer in the headlights. Even knowing what I now knew about her, I still couldn't quite reconcile the sight of her, unhinged like this, with the woman I'd known.

"Who the *fuck* are you?" Lindsey demanded, looking like she wasn't sure whether to laugh at her, or punch her in the stomach.

Florence was already charging towards the staircase. Lindsey ran after her, grabbing her arm and dragging her back. "Whoa, whoa, whoa there, crazy. Just where exactly do you think you're going?"

Florence fought and twisted, her eyes dangerously wild. "I have to talk to him," she insisted. "I have to talk to Daniel. He'll want to see me."

"Maddy, call the cops." Lindsey was maintaining a vice grip. "I don't think Danny needs to talk to you, honey."

"*DANIEL!*" Flo shrieked, loud enough to make me flinch. The bedroom door popped open a few moments later.

The look on his face was priceless.

He thundered down the stairs, wearing just his pajama pants, but still managing to look incredibly threatening. I actually took a step back as he reached the main floor, snatching Flo's arm away from his sister's grasp and staring her down.

"*What are you doing here?*" he snarled, his chest rising and falling quickly with every breath.

"I just needed to see you," said Flo, very sweetly, her attitude completely changed. "Your friend here let me right in."

"I'm his *sister*," said Lindsey, frostily. "And I was expecting a pizza."

Flo was giving him the puppy-dog face; it made me feel vaguely sick to my stomach. "I just want to talk to you, Dan. Please. Don't make me do something I'll regret."

Daniel's jaw twitched. "I'm not afraid of you," he said.

"Oh, really?" Flo's eyes flickered to Lindsey. "Does she already know?"

"There's nothing to know," said Daniel, through clenched teeth.

"Sure, I guess you're right," Florence replied, still looking at Lindsey. "Assuming you're aware that his marriage is a fake."

Lindsey closed her eyes for a minute, letting out a long, deep sigh.

"Of course I know," she said. "I'm his *big sister*, you lunatic."

Now, everyone in the room was staring at her.

"We can talk about all that later," said Lindsey, with a dismissive gesture. "The important thing is, are you going to get the fuck out of here and leave him alone for the rest of your natural life? Because if not, you're going to buy yourself a world of hurt."

"Fine," Florence spat. Daniel let her go, roughly, and she slunk towards the door. "I hope you're very happy together."

And with that, she was gone.

Lindsey slammed and locked the door behind her.

"Unbelievable," she said.

"Why didn't you tell me?" Daniel demanded, walking towards her. "It would have saved everyone a lot of trouble."

"I don't know," Lindsey replied, indignant. "Does it matter? You're the one with the fake fucking marriage, little brother."

"I can't *believe* you," said Daniel, but there was no real hostility in his voice.

"I can't believe *you*," she countered. "Lying to your own sister. You should know by now that it never works. Anybody with half a brain can put the pieces together."

"Well, for your information, I've got my citizenship now."

"Good for you. You can fool the government, but you can't fool me. Just keep that in mind, okay?"

She turned and began walking towards her room, but stopped halfway there and turned to look at both of us.

"Oh - by the way - you two realize you're really in love with each other, right?"

After she shut the guest room door behind her, Daniel turned to me. "Ignore her," he said. "She's just trying to obnoxious."

I stared at him. "That's what you feel compelled to comment on? Really?"

"What else is there to say?"

I didn't actually have an answer for him.

The buzzer went off again.

"That's got to be the pizza, this time," I said.

Daniel looked through the peep-hole carefully before he opened the door.

Once the pizza was paid for, he dropped it on the coffee table and sat down, opening the box and reaching for a slice. "Lindsey won't mind, as long as we leave some for her," he said.

"Stress eating?" I teased, taking a slice for myself.

"No," he replied, indignantly, around a mouthful of cheese.

To this day, I'll never know what possessed me to say the next thing that popped out of my mouth.

"You know, the last time we had pizza together it didn't really end well."

"I'm aware," he said, drily.

We both chewed in silence for a moment.

"I know this doesn't mean much now," he

said, "but if I had the chance to start over with this, I'd do things differently."

"And marry someone else?" I suggested. He didn't say no - but he didn't say yes, either.

"I let the whole thing go to my head," he said, after a while. "I actually thought..."

My fingers tightened around the pizza crust I was holding. "You actually thought...?" I prompted.

He shook his head. "No - no, I'm sorry. I shouldn't have said anything. I've put you in enough unenviable situations as it is."

"Hey," I said, gently. "I've had a great time, being your wife." I thought of the interview, and our fight. "Well...most of the time."

He laughed a little. "That's very kind of you to say."

"I don't just want to walk away from it prematurely," I went on. "I mean, you know...in case something else comes up."

He shut his eyes for a moment, and then spoke again. "I'm sorry I called you selfish," he said. "I'm the selfish one. I have been from the beginning. You've been very sweet, and kind, and tolerant of the most awkward situation possible. I appreciate everything you've done. I really do. But Maddy-" he hesitated, and took a deep breath. "I can't be around you anymore."

My pulse was thumping deafeningly in my ears. "Why not?"

"Do I really have to spell it out for you?" He looked at me, a little disbelieving.

"I'd really appreciate it," I said, my voice sounding very distant.

"I like you," he said, simply. "That's all. Better than anyone I've ever *really* dated. I thought it would be all right, at first - lend an air of authenticity to the whole thing. Couldn't possibly hurt for me to be little bit smitten, could it?"

I pinched myself.

"Ow," I said.

He stared at me. "Did you just pinch yourself?"

"No," I said. "Are you being serious right now?"

"Of course I am," he said, gently. "I'm sorry, I thought it was obvious."

"It was.....not," I said. "Obvious. Not at all."

"Well," he said. "This is awkward."

I laughed. I had to.

"So, what...you thought I knew, and I was just toying with your emotions to get in your pants?"

"It doesn't sound very sensible," he said slowly, "when you put it like that."

"It doesn't sound very sensible no matter what," I said. "Why on earth would you be so paranoid?"

"Wait, wait," he said. "So if you weren't

toying with me - what, then?"

My throat constricted. "What do you mean?"

"Do you...are you..."

I'd never seen him at such a complete loss for words before. "Relax," I said, finally, putting him out of his misery. "I...I like you, too."

Being perfectly honest, the word "like" didn't even begin to cover it. But I wasn't going to let myself go there. Not just yet.

"Maddy..." He looked at me with an expression that was some strange mix of hope and trepidation, mixed with relief, mixed with...

"Hey," I said. "Let's not get too carried away. We've known each other for what...eight months?"

"And yet, you're my wife."

Such simple words, coming out of his mouth - but suddenly, they took on a whole new meaning.

"I know," I said. "But all the same."

"All the same," he agreed, his shoulders relaxing a little.

I leaned back on the sofa and rested against him, letting his arm drape over my shoulders. Just like a real couple. And for once, that thought didn't come with a side of heartache.

"Oh - Maddy?" he said, after a long silence.

I stirred. "Yeah?"

"Please don't tell my sister," he said. "She'll

never shut up about being right."

The guest room door popped open. "I heard that, you jackass."

Epilogue

I woke up slowly, to the sun peeking in through the blinds. Stirring in bed, I realized I was wrapped up in a tight embrace.

"Good morning," Daniel murmured in my ear. I smiled, slowly.

"G'morning," I managed, as he pressed soft, insistent kisses on the side of my face. I rolled over to face him, not even protesting when he kissed me on the mouth - that was a fight I'd given up long ago, once I was confident that when he said he didn't care about my morning breath, he really, *really* meant it.

The scarlet rope was still coiled up on the floor where we'd left it, after last night's activities. Over time, it had grown more smooth and supple, curling around my body like a second skin. I remembered how it had made me feel, mere hours before - how *he*had made me feel - and I shivered against the heat of his skin.

His fingers drifted along my body with a feather-light touch, igniting a slow fire deep inside. I was still sore from last night, but apparently I hadn't gotten enough. I made a quiet, encouraging *hmmm* as his hand dipped lower.

I thought he'd known just how to touch me the first time we were together, but he'd only gotten better at reading my body and giving me what I wanted, often before I even knew what it was.

His fingers slipped between my folds, teasing me. Testing me.

I slid my leg up over his hip, spreading myself open. He smiled, and I felt his hardness nudge against me. I was still sleepy, but my body was wide awake and ready. I tilted my head back as he slid into me - agonizingly slow, but so perfectly satisfying.

He filled me up just the same as he'd always done, but the feeling of skin on skin was still new, still intoxicating. I rolled my hips with his movements. He reached down to caress me, his fingers rubbing slow circles just where I needed them. I let out a small noise, my eyelids going heavy. He'd hit the sweet spot, and he knew it. He was watching my expressions carefully, our faces so close that our noses were almost touching.

Sometimes we played games - ropes and handcuffs, pretending to be people that we weren't. Sometimes he would bring me to the edge and then pull me back, again and again, just to assert himself, to remind me that I could control my own body if he demanded it of me. And I had grown to love those games. As frustrating as they could be, they comforting. Dependable. Intimate.

But sometimes, there were no games.

Sometimes it was just us, with no artifice. No mitigations or apologies. I wouldn't necessarily say that I preferred one way to the other, but it was awfully nice to have both.

This morning, it was just us.

He was my husband, not my billionaire boss who'd once tried to buy a year of my life. That was our past. Until recently, our future had been unsure. But now, it was clear there was no longer any need for a contract to keep us together.

I melted into his touch, breathless and quivering in his arms. I'd never understood how he could reduce me to this with just the slow, steady rhythm of his hand - but I certainly wasn't about to complain.

Then, just like that, I shattered. Somewhere in the midst of the mind-numbing pleasure, I felt him thrust deep inside me, one last time, his open mouth connecting with my shoulder, teeth sinking in just far enough to leave a red mark.

When I blinked back to life, Daniel was smiling and stroking my hair. He kissed the tip of my nose, and I made a face.

"Happy anniversary," he said, his voice still gravelly from sleep.

I grinned. "Has it been a year already?"

"I know," he replied, lightly grabbing a handful of my hair. "It's a shame, isn't it? I don't own you anymore."

"We'll just have your lawyer draft up something new," I said.

He chuckled, pulling me close and kissing my forehead.

"I love you, sweetheart."

"I love you too," I muttered, against his chest.

I closed my eyes, and just breathed.

ABOUT THE AUTHOR

Melanie Marchande is a young writer who loves creating fun, flirty, and occasionally steamy stories about two people realizing they just can't live without each other. She loves hearing from readers, so makes sure to connect with her online:

MelanieMarchande.com
MelanieMarchande.Tumblr.com
Facebook.com/MelanieMarchande
Twitter.com/MellieMarchande
MelanieMarchande@gmail.com

And join her mailing list for exclusive freebies, updates, and giveaways:
eepurl.com/srHcH

Loved the book? Melanie Marchande is part of Insatiable Reads Book Tours (insatiablereads.com), where the hottest authors in romance debut their sizzling new reads! As one of our author's readers, you qualify for the Insatiable Reads VIP newsletter: sign up and you'll be notified of new releases, giveaways and discounts before anyone else! Go to:
eepurl.com/vNTjP

To see the blue-and-white necklace and earrings set that is featured in the book, along with many other beautiful handmade pieces, visit Youphoric on Etsy: etsy.com/shop/youphoric

39604918R00144

Made in the USA
Lexington, KY
02 March 2015